BENEATH AN OUTBACK SKY

Sophie Nash's outback pastoral station in South Australia's panoramic Flinders Ranges is in danger of going under, unless she can find another source of revenue. So when charismatic geologist Charlie Kendall arrives to camp on her property with his students, love is the last thing on her mind. In fact, Sophie has seen personal loss devastate her family and has vowed never to lose her heart. But Charlie's charms are hard to resist, and his family might just have the solution to her problems . . .

NOELENE JENKINSON

◆

BENEATH AN OUTBACK SKY

Complete and Unabridged

LINFORD
Leicester

First published in Great Britain in 2014

First Linford Edition
published 2016

A catalogue record for this book is available
from the British Library.

ISBN 978–1–4448–2730–9

Published by
F. A. Thorpe (Publishing)
Anstey, Leicestershire

Set by Words & Graphics Ltd.
Anstey, Leicestershire
Printed and bound in Great Britain by
T. J. International Ltd., Padstow, Cornwall

This book is printed on acid-free paper

Sophie Nash turned and regarded the view behind her. Thanks to permanent springs, the Casuarina Downs homestead, with its solid limestone walls and shady veranda, was a world of calm and grace in an oasis of lavender hedges, green lawns and shade. She felt privileged to be part-owner of this outback sheep station in South Australia's Flinders Ranges.

She turned back to her purpose: confronting her partner, Jack Bryce. Taking a deep breath, she raised her hand and knocked on the whitewashed door of his historic original stone cottage on the property. His old scuffed boots sat on the front step.

Jack answered. She studied his overlong wavy chestnut hair, suntanned good looks and stubbled jaw. His trademark cheeky smile was missing today. In recent times, a subtle change had taken place between them. She hated that their former uncomplicated mateship of ten years was now floundering. Without a word, he stepped back into the room. This meeting had been prearranged, and Sophie suspected it might end in harsh words and raised voices. She entered and closed the door.

She glanced around his main living room, one of only four in the historic building. Multi-paned windows admitted the gloomy afternoon light. Deep chairs and sofas sat around an earth-toned rug on the stone floor. Outback and automotive magazines were piled on a side table together with a pack of cigarettes. He withdrew one and struck a match to it, the ritual filling the strain between them.

Sophie rarely ventured here because loner Jack prized his privacy — the cause of their present discord.

'I've just been on the phone to the bank manager. Again.' Jack was a rough diamond and she would trust him with her life, but he could be as stubborn as an angry old bull baulking at a cattle race. When there was no response, she continued. 'Not looking good.' She sank her hands into her jeans pockets and leant against the wall.

'And?'

'Same old. Hounding for more payments.' She eyed him grimly. 'Our financial situation is not just getting desperate. It's already there.' She pulled a wry grin, trying to lighten the situation.

'Season's shaping up to be a good one. Wool clip after shearing should balance the books.'

'After a string of bad seasons? Barely. I see the bank statements, Jack. I should know. I'm not exaggerating.' She paused before adding carefully, 'I wish you'd take more of an interest.'

He grinned. 'You know I'd rather be outdoors.'

'So would I, but we need to keep this station profitable. We've been in the red for two years now. The bank won't stay patient forever. Bottom line, we need cash flow besides the annual wool cheque or we lose this place, Jack,' she said with a sigh. 'And we both know how to achieve it.'

'You know I'm against tourism.'

'And I'm explaining that our circumstances are dire and we need it. Most other properties in these beautiful ranges have already embraced it to value-add and are reaping the rewards,' Sophie told him. 'I believe the time has come when we at least have to give it a try.'

'No.'

'Just for a year,' she pleaded. 'A trial.'

Jack drew heavily on his cigarette and blew out the smoke. 'I'm not having people invading our land.'

'Exactly, Jack. *Our* land. It's mine, too. Not just yours,' she pointed out. He stayed silent and glared. 'Maybe if *you* juggled the books and dealt with the bank, you'd appreciate the bad state we're in.' Sophie's voice rose with her frustration. She had heeded Jack's demands for too long and delayed the inevitable. But time had expired. The manager's alarming words of warning still rang in her ears. He had hinted against carrying them beyond this year. She hadn't worked and saved hard for ten years toward a dream of owning her own property just to have it wrenched away by an impatient bank and an obstinate business partner. It was time to stand and fight.

'We've already had travel agencies asking us to consider overnight accommodation in the homestead, and the University of Adelaide has approached us for two years running now to permit student geology camps on the property.'

Oh how she'd been tempted by those generous financial offers, but forced to sit on her hands and refuse because of Jack's stance on the idea. Sophie called it progress. Jack called it an intrusion.

'We let them in or lose Casuarina Downs, Jack. Simple as that.' Sophie straightened and folded her arms. 'One trial visit, Jack, please, and see how it goes?' she begged when he just glowered and stalled. 'We could try the university first,' she pressed her advantage when he showed a spark of interest. 'They only want access to camp by the billabong and permission to fossick for two weeks. We'd never see them.'

Jack studied her calmly. It was the first time she had even advanced this far in having him listen and trying to persuade him to change his mind. She sighed and to nudge his decision, half-turned for the door. 'We don't have the luxury of waiting any longer, Jack. Not this time. The alternative is to start selling our flocks, relinquish the lease and move on. Do you want that?' she pushed, knowing he wouldn't fancy the idea any more than she did. It had taken too long to get this far.

Sophie held her breath and it seemed forever before he blew out a cloud of impatient smoke, glowered and said curtly, 'One year.'

Her joy exploded like fireworks. 'You agree?'

He scowled and pretended to look fierce, but she knew him better. He was a softie underneath. Then he nodded.

Sophie squealed and flung her arms around his neck in an ecstatic hug. 'Thank you, Jack. I promise we won't regret it.'

She was out the cottage door and streaking across the yard back to the homestead before Jack could change his mind. She didn't need to look up the university telephone number because she had memorised it. Just in case.

★   ★   ★

Three weeks later Sophie whistled to her favourite kelpie, Drover. He bounded around the corner of the house at the sound of her boots on the veranda flagstones. She smiled and returned his loyalty with the usual vigorous morning rub of his head and scratch behind the ears.

'Morning, fella.'

She stretched. It was good to get outdoors again after staring at a computer screen in the office for a couple of hours catching up on station bookwork. Besides, the imbalance between the red and black figures was depressing. She squinted against the mid-morning sun now risen above the surrounding ranges and shielded her eyes to where clouds of dust heralded the new arrivals. They must have left Adelaide before sunup, because it was a four-hour drive out here.

She snatched her black Akubra from one of the pegs on the outside wall by the back door and patted her thigh. 'Let's go meet our visitors, eh, boy?'

Her mood and steps were light. Knowing intruders were expected, Jack had vanished into the hills. Sophie zipped her padded vest against the chill spring breeze and crunched across the broad gravelled drive to wait.

★　★　★

Dr. Charles Kendall focused on driving despite the chatter among his three young fellow passengers. It had been dark when they left the city but the morning sun now streamed in the vehicle windows. From time to time he removed his glasses and rubbed his weary eyes. They had stopped once to stretch and inhale the crisp air, making him realise how much he missed the bush. He checked the rear-view mirror to make sure the minivan still followed with the other students who had applied to participate for this fieldwork trip in their half-semester spring holidays.

Even in the company of his talkative students, Charlie tried to ignore the emptiness that hit him these days. Until recently, he had never seriously considered settling down. He had come pretty close with Belle, but as soon as he had mentioned his love of the country and the possibility of living somewhere beyond suburbia, she had promptly ended their relationship.

He kicked himself that he should have known her better and read the signs. In hindsight, their parting was fortunate. Better to discover incompatibilities sooner rather than later. She had seemed so right and he'd got it so wrong. He might be able to read rocks, but he'd failed to read a woman.

Caught up in reflections, Charlie almost missed the property sign to Casuarina Downs, braked and turned off through wide stone entrance posts onto an avenue of gum trees that led to their destination.

* * *

Sophie watched the approaching vehicles cross the homestead paddock. A silver four-wheel drive with a sunroof and black spoked wheels, hauling a covered camping trailer, came into view and pulled up. *Nice ride*.

A tall man wearing glasses and older than herself peeled himself out from behind the wheel in the driver's seat and stretched. Although clean-shaven, his rugged appearance and weathered face suggested an outdoor life. That figured. He was a geologist after all. Checked shirt, moleskins and sports coat with leather elbow patches — rather smart for fossicking. She trusted his dress code was more practical for work.

Three younger passengers emerged wearing, jeans, hoodies and sneakers. Minutes later a following minivan drew up alongside, from which the remaining students gradually tumbled.

The man ran a hand through his light brown wavy hair, squinted behind his glasses and slowly surveyed his surroundings. Sophie moved forward and extended a hand in greeting.

'Good morning. I'm Sophie Nash and this is Drover,' she said warmly, patting her dog. 'Dr. Kendall?'

His big brown hand grabbed hers and squeezed. 'Charlie.' The voice was deep and friendly. With hands on hips that pushed his coat back, he nodded toward the hovering students. 'And this is the rest of the crew.'

'Welcome to Casuarina Downs.'

* * *

The woman was a similar height to his own, Charlie noted when his gaze locked onto hers at eye level. He tried not to stare. Their host was a tall agile blonde, hair pulled back at the nape underneath a wide black hat, its brim casting half her face into shadow. The long sleeves of a pink striped shirt with the collar up peeped out from beneath a snugly zipped vest. Tight blue jeans hugged her body and her feet were planted slightly apart in shiny black boots.

The woman was comfortable with herself and clearly belonged to this country. Probably born out here. But he shouldn't be looking at another woman with even the slightest interest. Since Belle had dumped him, he was still smarting from the rejection and nursing some heavily wounded male pride.

Sophie turned toward the house. 'If you'll follow me into the homestead, our housekeeper Alice has morning tea in the kitchen, then I'll lead you out to your campsite.'

The company straggled into the large country kitchen in the French provincial style that Sophie adored, with its gleaming white and timber combinations. All eyes focused on the sliced cinnamon-apple teacake, Devonshire tea, platters of fresh sandwiches and hot savouries laid out on the central island bench. Kettles simmered on the Rayburn cooker that pushed its warmth into the room.

'This is Alice Johnston,' Sophie introduced her Aboriginal cook fondly. The shy woman's wide smile revealed two crooked front teeth. 'Your camp is self-catering but I've arranged with the university to provide one campfire meal during your stay — a spit roast with damper — and we'll host a farewell barbeque before you leave.'

Murmurs of appreciation rippled through the group, then everyone fell to eating. Quiet Kendall nursed a huge mug of tea and demolished a slice of cake. His steady gazes were intimidating.

Sophie edged closer. 'Dr. Kendall — '

'Charlie,' he interrupted softly.

'Charlie.' She pulled a quick smile. It felt too personal using his Christian name, although she was on first-name terms with everyone else out here. 'Let me know when you want to leave later for the campsite. It's only a half-hour drive out along the ridge and down into the gully by the billabong.'

'Can't wait to see it.'

'The camping ground is flat so it's ideal for pitching tents.'

'You live out here alone with just Alice?' he asked abruptly.

'No. I have a partner, Jack Bryce, but he'll be scarce. Not into people,' she quickly explained when his gaze clouded. 'And we employ seasonal workmen, especially shearers around November. The hills are good wool-growing country. In a favourable year,' she rambled nervously as Kendall stared intently like she was some kind of rock specimen.

'And a draw for scientists like us. The ridge formations are hundreds of millions of years old. These ranges provide the best display in the world of geological formations.'

'Sounds like you're going to enjoy your stay,' she said wryly.

'Plus it's a beautiful landscape,' Kendall acknowledged.

Sophie eyed him curiously. 'People don't often consider it so.' She released a long sigh. 'But I couldn't imagine living anywhere else now.'

'So, where else have you lived?' he asked, his head engagingly tilted, his big brown eyes engaging hers from behind the glasses.

'Born in Western Australia, been a jillaroo in Queensland and the Territory, was in mining management amongst iron ore up in the Pilbara, and headed overseas for a spell.'

'Sounds like you've had an adventurous life so far.'

'I hear you guys dig up rocks all over the world.'

He nodded. 'I've managed India, Turkey and the Mediterranean, but never this part of the outback.' His mouth edged into that appealing grin again. 'I suspect my school holidays down on my grandparents' farm on the Fleurieu don't count.'

Sophie contemplated his mention of the emerald triangular peninsula that jutted into the ocean down south. If she hadn't been outback born and bred, she might even envy the rich pastureland and its high rainfall.

'At least it's green down there. You live in Adelaide, I presume?'

He nodded. 'My parents and married sister all live in the hills. I live on the beach. For the moment,' he replied swiftly. He glanced reflectively out through the large kitchen windows then turned back to her. 'What decided you on settling here away from family?'

This was like the Spanish Inquisition. But his interest seemed genuine, if unsettling, because he was digging, so she relented and shared. 'After a decade of sleeping in swags under the stars and some pretty basic outback living quarters, I felt like a little more comfort and the need to put down roots.' The admission wasn't easily made because the urge in recent years had caught her by surprise.

'Your partner Jack from around here?' He tried to make his question sound casual, but she sensed her reply mattered.

'No. He's from the Territory.'

Kendall leaned back against a kitchen counter and folded his arms. 'Parents?'

Sophie cringed. She hated when personal questions grew too close. 'Mother, yes.' She paused and her voice softened. 'My father died over a decade ago now.'

With his sharply perceptive gaze

locked onto hers, Charlie picked up on her change of tone and frowned. 'He must have been quite young.'

His comment triggered her usual reluctance to confide and memories Sophie preferred to forget. To cover the hurt, she steeled herself and said in a low, cool voice, 'He was a great bloke and a decent father. He didn't deserve to die so soon.'

Charlie pushed himself away from the bench and held up his hands. 'Sorry. Didn't mean to pry.' He tactfully backed off and moved away toward his group. 'Okay guys, time to move out.'

He barely raised his commanding voice but the students heard and complied. Watching them leave the kitchen, Sophie regretted her sharp response to him. Grief over the loss of her father still wrenched. With a straight back and emotional shield safely back in place again, she trailed after the visitors.

Out on the veranda, she whistled for Drover, avoiding Charlie's curious puzzled expression, and said, 'I'll meet you all out front.' She pulled a quick tight smile in a display of toughness to cover her emotional scars.

Drover trotted at her booted heels and leapt into the back of her gleaming white utility. She checked the rifle on the seat alongside was on safety, gunned the deep throbbing engine and drove around the homestead to join the others. As it rumbled to an idling halt, the students tossed her glances of admiration and amazement.

'Serious wheels,' one said, respectfully eyeing the front bull bar and UHF radio aerials sticking up on either side of the cab.

'Like the note,' another commented.

'Jack modified the sports exhaust for me.' She smiled.

'Sounds like an indispensable guy,' Charlie said wryly as he examined her vehicle.

Who was he to question her choice of mates? Sophie flung out a defiant challenge. 'He's reliable. Out here you need to be able to trust and depend on your mates.'

'You camping out with us?' another asked, indicating her bedroll in the back of the vehicle.

'No. My swag lives permanently in the ute for emergencies only. These days I prefer the comfort of a good night's sleep indoors. Jack thinks I'm getting soft.' She laughed and glanced around the group. 'If you're all ready, let's head out.'

Charlie was already walking back to his vehicle. His disinterest sparked a twinge of disappointment that she stifled as she led the convoy out to the back track, along the ridge and down into a deep gully covered with cypress pines and the casuarinas that gave the property its name. The beautiful idyllic campsite opened out beside a waterhole fringed with reeds and sedges, overhung with red river gum trees and surrounded by steep red hills.

When they were all out of their vehicles, Charlie took in the scenery and, assuming his leadership role, squinted skyward as he addressed his students.

'Look up, guys, at these ancient mountain ranges.' His voice echoed around the billabong. 'You can see by the rock strata of this rugged escarpment that the gorge is set against the slabs of an ancient sea floor that was thrust up.'

Hands planted on hips, his voice quietly lowered and deepened, assuming a respectful awe. 'Millions of years of rain and sun have carved it into this furrowed landscape. The layers of time are horizontal and have been exposed by weathering.' His gaze narrowed as he turned to Sophie. 'Perhaps Miss Nash has some local knowledge to add.'

Behind the glasses and standing close, Sophie noted a pair of engaging dark brown eyes. She jammed her hands into her vest pockets and took up his challenge.

'These ranges were first settled by pastoralists about one hundred and fifty years ago. Then came the miners seeking the copper outcrops, but the hills didn't produce much metal and the mines were soon abandoned. This billabong was their watering point before heading into the ranges. Their biggest problem was transport and finding water. The railways developed and wells were sunk but life was still hard. The gorges rarely have flowing water in them. This permanent water-hole is an exception and fed from a spring.

'While I have your attention,' she continued, 'I'd like to take the opportunity to remind you of the area's isolation. There's no mobile phone reception out here but I'm sure you're equipped with UHF radios.'

She glanced to Charlie for confirmation and he nodded. Sophie turned back to the group.

'The repeater towers work on line-of-sight. If you need a better signal move to higher ground. Naturally I hope you don't have one during your stay but, in an emergency, identify who you are, where you are and what's wrong. Remember you're on a public network so keep it short and polite.'

She smiled to soften the warning. 'As for venturing further on the property, leave gates as you find them, stay on the tracks and don't disturb any animals or watering points. Good luck with your explorations and enjoy your stay.'

A light patter of applause accompanied Sophie as she left the group and approached Charlie. 'I'll contact you in a week to arrange the camp meal.'

'I look forward to it,' he murmured absently, his previous warmth seemingly cooled.

Sophie dragged her attention away from the compelling unreadable man, whistled for Drover who reappeared and leapt into the back of the ute, and drove away. Baffled by Kendall's hot and cold attitude, she determined not to be distracted by any man and focused instead on the large and timely electronic payment sent by the university and already safely deposited into the station bank account.

* * *

After a busy week moving sheep in from the ranges to paddocks closer to the woolshed ready for shearing in the coming weeks, Sophie and Jack returned to the homestead and cottage to clean up.

She had contacted Charlie at the geology campsite yesterday and made arrangements for the cookout. To her own personal confusion, at the sound of his voice on the radio she had grown warm and felt pleased that he once again sounded cordial. Idle thoughts of him had stayed with her all week.

Because Alice didn't drive, Jack had taken her out earlier to get the fire built up for cooking. He had fiercely resisted joining in. He didn't do crowds but somehow Sophie convinced him that a handful of young folk shouldn't pose any threat and he grudgingly caved.

Besides, she needed his physical help with loading

Freshened up, he reappeared in blue jeans with a wide leather belt, a clean white shirt and polished tan boots. He was one handsome man, Sophie admitted, but not for her. She had only ever considered him as a brother and a mate.

She whistled softly and flicked her eyebrows. 'Looking good, Bryce.'

As they heaved food boxes together, she noticed his gaze linger over the pink shirt she had tucked into her tight black jeans that encased her long legs and ended in her best pair of shiny black low-heeled boots. She had released her long blonde hair from its usual pony tail, brushed it out and it now drifted free over her shoulders.

'You look gorgeous,' he murmured huskily.

Sophie frowned and hesitated in surprise. Jack was your typical bush bloke and didn't usually flatter. His compliment startled her and sparked a light bulb moment. Surely not! She felt a twinge of guilt that she had been thinking of Charlie as she dressed, not Jack.

She deflected his remark with, 'Thanks. We need to put our best foot forward in case we decide to expand our tourism in the future, don't we?' she quickly suggested.

'Wish we didn't need them,' he muttered and the awkward moment passed.

'Well, the reality is we do, Jack. Especially in a bad season — or worse, a run of them like we've had. Now, let's head on out and show them a great night.'

They split up and each headed out to the campsite in separate vehicles because there wasn't enough room for all three of them to return later in Sophie's ute alone, though she supposed Jack would happily ride in the back.

The camp was deserted on arrival, but the week had wrought big changes to the area, Sophie noticed as she approached. Numerous tents had been erected, and a large central fireplace had been dug and circled with rocks. Alice had stoked up the coals for dinner. Geological gear littered the ground everywhere. Rock chisels, maps and leather satchels lay about with books on seats and coats hanging over the backs of camp chairs around the fire.

Not surprisingly, Alice was missing. The bush was her home and she often wandered off to explore, returning with interesting finds most other people might miss. Her campfire roared and sent out waves of heat into the cooling evening. Blue smoke curled up lazily into the trees. The camp was already shadowed as the sun sank behind the surrounding hills. Jack and Sophie unloaded the food-stuffs onto a long trestle table at one end set up for serving.

A short time later the camp occupants all began straggling back. Scruffy and weary but, judging by the smiles on faces and the buzz of enthusiastic conversation, everyone seemed cheerful.

Sophie met Charlie's gaze as he brought up the rear. He smiled across the camp and her heart leapt but she quickly turned away to finish setting up. But her attempt to disregard him didn't work.

Next thing, Charlie was at her side. 'You're a welcome sight.'

'That's probably because we bought food that isn't either dried in a packet or has come out of a tin,' she teased. 'Alice has prepared a feast for you all.' She kept the conversation professional.

The few females in the group disappeared into their tents to clean up but, despite the brisk evening air, the young men stripped down to shorts and braved a dip in the waterhole with noisy banter and splashing.

In her distraction at the crew returning and her suppressed delight at seeing Charlie again looking all rugged and appealing in dusty bush clothes with a few days' growth of stubble on his face, Sophie forgot to introduce Jack.

Charlie moved across to him and extended a hand in greeting. 'Charlie Kendall. I don't believe we've met.'

'Jack,' he said bluntly and continued working.

To cover her partner's rudeness and stimulate conversation, Sophie smiled at Charlie. 'Have a good week?'

'Excellent.' He beamed. 'I've worn them out so I'm granting them a day off tomorrow.'

'Great. Everything here okay?'

'Ideal.' He hesitated. 'Camping under canvas in good weather works fine, but if it was wet . . . ' He frowned and paused. 'I'm not so sure. Might be an option worth considering for the future,' Charlie suggested.

Although the weather forecast was favourable, you never could be sure, so Sophie considered his gentle hint and immediately thought of the shearers' quarters empty for eleven months of the year. 'There might be alternative accommodation back at the homestead, but it would mean a half-hour drive out here to the site every day.'

Charlie shrugged easily. 'Doesn't sound like too much of a problem. Could work.'

In a way, Sophie almost hoped Jack had overheard. It might save explanations later. He would be far from impressed if visitors lodged even closer to the homestead. Fact was, if this field camp trip worked out, the shearers' block was right next door to Jack's cottage that he had deliberately chosen for its solitude away from the homestead. In that case, she would need his agreement to proceed, and it seemed highly unlikely he would grant it. But the continued cash flow investment would mean a huge boost to their working economy and ease the financial pressures all around.

'Alice is out wandering the bush,' Charlie advised. 'We saw her as we were coming back.'

'Thought she might be.' Sophie smiled. 'She loves her country. It's important to her people. They possess a deep insight for it.'

Sophie had no sooner finished speaking than the camp cook reappeared. She smiled shyly and silently approached to lift the camp oven lids and check on the sizzling legs of lamb, adding a large dish of prepared vegetables to roast. Those who drifted about nearby watched in fascination as Alice raked the deep bed of coals back over the cast-iron camp ovens with the glowing red embers to finish cooking.

While they waited, pairs of young female eyes strayed in Jack's direction and lingered. His crisp white shirt offset his dark good looks, but the handsome man remained oblivious. Sophie felt like giving him a decent shake to wake him up to the world around him.

More than anything, she wished Jack greater happiness. Outwardly he appeared content enough, and they worked companionably together, but she knew there was an underlying emptiness; a vital element lacking in his life. A leftover result of his hard unloved childhood and the cause of his remote attitude, as if he deliberately kept most humanity at bay against further hurt. He allowed few people to get close.

Sophie joined the circle of students seated around the fire. 'Jack, come and join us,' she invited, looking back over her shoulder to where he sat apart from everyone else. Two of the girls glanced hopefully in his direction, but he only raised an arm in acknowledgement and stayed put.

Sophie predicted a discussion looming with her business partner. They had to agree on future plans and put them in place. Initially, years ago, their friendship had been fun and easy. These days it was growing strained.

Charlie slipped away to his tent on the edge of camp, so Sophie chatted to the students. 'So what have you guys been doing all week?'

'Exploring.'

'Having fun.'

'Discovering muscles we never had,' came the quick replies amid smiles and laughter.

'Sounds like you're all embracing it regardless. Why did you all choose to come on this trip?' she addressed the gathering in general.

'Field camp finishes off our under-grad training,' one said.

'It's a beautiful place to learn,' another young man added, sitting forward in his chair, hands resting on his knees. He'd been the one who particularly admired her ute on arrival.

'The Flinders do tend to seep into your soul,' Sophie agreed.

'We're learning so much stuff,' one young woman enthused. 'And the doc's a great teacher.' Judging by the adoration in the girl's eyes, Sophie guessed any young female would be easily captivated by his gentlemanly charm. After all, hadn't she, too?

'We're learning how to check out the

surroundings to consider the geological implications,' the girl continued. 'To know where to explore in the first place you need to understand an area's geology. Types of rocks. How they were laid down.'

'I'm just glad to ditch the classroom so we can apply our training in the field.'

'Yeah. Beats the indoors any day. We get to use our field gear, collect samples, draft maps.'

'Not to mention walking and climbing,' one young woman groaned. 'For kilometres.'

'Vehicles only go so far in these ranges,' Sophie sympathised.

'That food is starting to smell pretty darn good, Alice,' one lad chided, and a ripple of laughter ran around the circle as the cook approached to check on the meal.

'Be ready soon,' she said, grinning bashfully.

'Sure whips up an appetite scrambling around all day, chipping at rocks.'

'At least you work as hard as you can talk, Ben.' Charlie emerged quietly from the shadows, hands sunk into his pockets, grinning. He sported fresh clothes: a checked shirt, moleskins and loafers.

'Hey Doc,' the students chorused warmly.

The frivolous mood sobered a little with Charlie's appearance. To Sophie's surprise, he drew up a chair beside her. 'It's been a productive week for all of us,' he murmured, 'thanks to this exciting environment.'

When he grinned, Sophie melted. His dark brown eyes flashed and she almost forgot he wore glasses. They became part of him. 'You're welcome. Pleased the land is proving exciting as well as useful.'

His kind words reinforced their purpose in sharing this beautiful country and the tidy sums that could keep the station solvent, supplementing their working capital and lifting profits. Not to mention reducing that nasty overdraft. But sitting beside Charlie before a billabong campfire on a crisp spring evening, it was difficult to think of the geology group's visit as purely business. It was heartening to share what they owned. If only Jack could see its value and purpose to others.

'The students need hands-on training,' Charlie explained. 'Field camps are like a right of passage from being a student apprentice to becoming a self reliant geologist. It's vital before their employment so they experience all aspects of the career they choose.'

After the familiar pink colours of a Ranges sunset spread across the sky, dusk settled in and the usual chill of day's end at this time of year made the fire's radiant heat welcome. The first stars sparkled. Every now and then an owl called out into the quiet night.

'Aren't we behaving ourselves?' Charlie leaned confidentially closer.

Sophie jumped and frowned at the sound of his voice interrupting her thoughts and the peace, puzzling over what he meant.

'Jack's not looking happy back there,' he elaborated.

'Oh.' Sophie felt a curl of irritation that she needed to explain her partner's behaviour and dearly wished he was a more sociable type. 'I told you, he's not into crowds.'

Unless people knew Jack — and folk rarely did, simply because he didn't let them in — they could never fully understand him. It had even taken her, a good mate allowed to get closer than most, a decade to peep through the cracks. If she had learned anything, she believed Jack Bryce needed exactly what he shunned: a family. You had to let people get close to achieve that.

Even as she spoke, her mind pondered how that would work if tourism developed on the station as she hoped. Sophie couldn't see how Casuarina Downs could survive without it. Everything rode on Jack's cooperation. Feeling uncomfortable for having spoken so sharply and honestly to Charlie, silence fell between them. Perhaps Charlie also sensed her defensive loyalty.

Finally, the subject of her thoughts came forward. Jack helped Alice remove the lamb roasts and vegetables from the camp ovens. Sophie rescued the dampers cooking in foil in the coals. Alice carved the meat, sliced the still-warm and steaming bush bread, and then nodded to Sophie.

'Dinner, everyone,' she called out. 'Please come and help yourselves.'

Everyone filed along the food table, filled their plates and retired to their chairs around the fire to eat. Not surprisingly, conversation lapsed for a while as the gathering enjoyed the benefits of their cook's labours.

Later Sophie helped Alice to wash and clean up. One of the male students produced a guitar. They listened as they worked while he strummed and broke easily into the haunting melodies of some country-music love songs.

Meanwhile, Jack carted the crates and boxes back to his ute. Returning, he asked Sophie with hopeful warmth, 'Coming home?'

She glanced back toward the group, her loyalties split. She didn't want to hurt or reject Jack, but Charlie's profile was reflected in the firelight, his manner relaxed. The pull of his powerful physical presence raised a confusing need that compelled her to stay. She didn't feel ready to return to the homestead just yet.

'I'm staying on for a while. You take Alice.'

She laid a gentle hand on his arm to soften her refusal. A flash of disappointment crossed his face but he gave a quick smile and walked away. Once, not too long ago, she would have readily agreed, bidden their visitors goodnight and risen to join him.

Her booted feet carried her slowly back over to the campfire. Charlie noticed her approach and made a space beside him. Bless him. If he'd ignored her she would have felt crushed. Although she denied it to herself, he was the reason she wanted to stay.

When the billy boiled and they sipped mugs of tea, Charlie said, 'Hope it's okay, but since the kids are free tomorrow they've hinted they'd like to visit the more distant hills. You okay with them exploring the property further?'

'Sure.' She paused. 'I'm happy to show you all around if you like,' she suggested.

Charlie hesitated. 'To be honest, I think they need some space. I'm going to let them head out independently in the van without the doc looking over their shoulders.' He considered her at length then ventured, 'I was going to hang around camp and do some paperwork, but I'm happy to take you up on your offer though.'

Sophie was stunned and yet excited by his unexpected proposal.

'Unless it interferes with your station work,' Charlie hinted when she hesitated. Jack wouldn't mind?' he probed.

'No! I can spare half a day.' She shrugged easily to conceal her pleasure.

She caught her breath at the deep, meaningful glance he settled over her. A most revealing glance. Almost like relief. It was only then she suddenly realised Charlie had thought she and Jack were a romantic item.

To set him straight, Sophie looked directly into those warm brown eyes behind the glasses and emphasised clearly, 'Jack's my *business* partner. Nothing more,' she confirmed softly, scared of her growing attraction to this man but brave enough to spend time with him now the opportunity presented itself.

It was only a few hours. Her heart wasn't in any danger, was it? Neither she nor Jack rarely allowed themselves the luxury of some time off. She convinced herself that a few hours outdoors showcasing this land she had quickly grown to love would do her good.

Sophie cleared her throat. 'Afternoon

okay?' Charlie nodded. 'I'll swing by the camp before lunch then. Don't eat. Alice will pack a hamper.'

'You don't cook?' he teased.

'I barbeque. I'll show off my skills next week.'

The thought momentarily dulled their playful mood because it voiced the group's ultimate departure.

* * *

For more than one reason Sophie hardly slept that night, and next morning out on the veranda she braced herself as Jack strode across the yard from his cottage to the homestead where she waited. When she told him of her plans with Charlie, he bristled.

'We were supposed to move more sheep in from the north range.'

'I know, but we're ahead of schedule,' she said gently. 'I'll help you again tomorrow. Besides, I'll be up on the ridges. I'll keep an eye out for where the flocks are grazing.'

'Whatever you say, boss,' he threw at her, forcing a wry face, although she knew he was offended, before turning on his booted heels and striding away again.

Sophie stared after him and frowned. She didn't understand what had subtly changed lately to cause this constant strain in their friendship, usually so companionable.

With Jack's conflict gnawing at her mind, Sophie scooted out to meet the mail plane that arrived every Saturday morning. Many outback properties had a private airstrip, and Casuarina Downs was blessed with a suitable landing space with a natural surface east of the homestead block.

She watched the familiar low-slung Aero commander as it firstly appeared as a speck in the cloudy sky then gradually grew larger. The wind had picked up to gusty, but the plane descended easily and made a safe landing.

The pilot opened the door and

jumped down onto the ground carrying a small mail bag.

'Hi, Tony.' She tucked back a long strand of hair blown across her face.

'Soph,' he acknowledged, handing her the mail. 'Hey, Drover.' He affectionately patted the kelpie.

The animal, who was rarely far from his mistress, lapped up the extra attention then trotted off inquisitively around the plane. They yarned for a moment but Tony only ever stopped briefly before continuing onto other Flinders Ranges stations. His scheduled weekly run started at Port Augusta on the Gulf and covered countless outback properties and thousands of kilometres in a day, all the way to Queensland and back again. Often, any one of his three spare seats carried a paying passenger or two who came along for the experience and the ride. But not today.

Back at the homestead, Sophie sorted the mail in her office, including a personal envelope for Jack — unusual because he rarely received any. She noticed the familiar logo of Gulf River cattle station in the Territory where she and Jack had worked some years ago. It piqued her interest but she thought little more of it. She set it aside to hand on to him later.

She stopped off in her room to tidy her appearance before returning to the kitchen to load the lunch hamper, thermos and cooler bag Alice had prepared.

Drover was not amused to be left behind. 'Sorry, fella. Not today.' She patted him fondly, finding it hard to ignore the appeal in his eyes as he sat hopefully on his haunches even as she walked away.

As Sophie drove out to the geologists' field camp, she had already decided to showcase the property from its highest viewpoints and rocky outcrops to give Charlie a clear impression of the terrain both scenically and geologically. She thought he might appreciate that.

As her ute descended the track to the

waterhole, Charlie was waiting, standing alone in the empty camp. She reined in the buzz that kicked through her at the sight of him. He had proved quietly intriguing — for a city bloke. And she enjoyed his company. Amazing in itself, because Sophie deliberately discouraged male relationships.

As she walked toward Charlie now, he smiled. He was casually dressed today in cargos with their flaps and pockets, a long-sleeved black T-shirt hugging a muscled chest. Quite a change from her first glimpse of him when she wrongly labelled him strictly the studious type. Clearly, the glasses were misleading. Sophie was learning that Dr. Charles Kendall was not your average academic. He was no novice in the bush and hinted on arrival that his city living was not by choice. Idly, she wondered where he would rather be.

They sized each other up, Sophie in her jeans, trademark pink polo shirt and black Akubra.

46

'Afternoon,' she greeted. 'All set?'

He nodded. 'Looking forward to it. Are you sure I don't need to bring anything?'

'Nope. Fully equipped, so we can head out.'

Charlie eased his large frame into the passenger seat beside her. 'A woman and her ute eh?' He grinned in amusement at the spotless interior of the vehicle with touches of pink, revealing a feminine side to Sophie she preferred to keep hidden.

She knew he was teasing and liked his quiet sense of humour, reminiscent of her brother Dusty. 'Utes, quad bikes and four-wheel drives are more practical out here. But I'm guessing you already know that, since your profession gets you outdoors.'

She wound her way back up to the ridge top and snaked her way along the narrow rocky track. Spread out for tens of kilometres either side were the red craggy cliff faces of the Ranges sweeping up from the tree line that ran along the often dry creek beds into the foothills.

Soon they reached a lookout and stopped. They stood together as the wind whipped up from the shallow gorge below and silently absorbed the amazing panorama from the summit.

'It's cloudy today, but this gives you a great idea of the landscape we have out here. Being a geologist, you already know that.' She glanced at him, grinning. 'But if you look beyond the rocky country you see its hidden beauty. It's the little things.'

She found herself confiding to this appealing trustworthy man, hands anchored in her belt tabs, squinting skyward from beneath her broad hat as a wedge-tailed eagle wheeled past. 'Like that.' She paused to admire it. 'Some might think it inhospitable out here.' She turned to him again. 'But it's alive with plants and animals, and I stumble on something new or secret places every time I come out here that I never knew about before.'

Charlie shrugged and chuckled. 'I find all new terrain exciting. I look at it to analyse how old it is and how it was formed. It's certainly magnificent,' he agreed.

Standing in mutual silence, Sophie knew a moment of utter peace. Few people truly appreciated such harsh and isolated country, despite being only four hours from a capital city and on the fringes of more remote outback territory.

'To think this was all underwater once,' he murmured. 'The Flinders Ranges are the remains of a mountain chain thrust up from the sea five hundred million years ago. Erosion removed the softer rock, leaving your spectacular sculpted ridges. Imagine the fossils that must be buried under all this from the earliest forms of life on earth,' he marvelled in awe.

'Well I'll leave you to find them. I have enough trouble finding my sheep.'

Charlie threw back his head and laughed. Sophie was captivated by the sound carried away on the breeze, and the handsome light it spread across his face.

When he recovered, he added, 'The dry desert salt lake at the northern end of the Ranges up in Cameron's Corner where the three state borders meet is a fossil treasury.' He squinted, addressing Sophie but almost speaking to himself in reflection. 'Nineteenth-century scientists found giant fossil skeletons, petrified mangrove stumps and conifer logs up there. Evidence of a much wetter climate when the inland was a sea.'

Sophie grinned at Charlie's enthusiasm for his work and contemplated the information. 'Hard to imagine in the face of this semi-arid landscape. It makes our three score and ten years rather insignificant, doesn't it?'

'Certainly makes you consider your life and the earth around you in an entirely different light,' he murmured. 'Gives you a new appreciation for every day.'

Sophie warmed to not only his depth of knowledge but his perception of humanity and the fragility of life itself. 'The Ranges are mineral-rich, too. Amethysts. Pink and blue sapphires are apparently found here. Well,' she added, turning to her companion, 'there's a picnic spot further on. We'll only travel about forty kilometres today, but it will take a few hours,' she continued as they headed back to the ute. 'Our night skies are free of light pollution and our nearest small town is over one hundred kilometres away, so astronomers love it,' Sophie said as she unpacked the picnic hamper from the back of the ute.

Charlie tossed her a cheeky glance. 'Not too much out here that I don't love myself.'

And he wasn't looking at the scenery as he spoke, Sophie noticed, but directly at her instead!

She found such a compliment from this quietly sexy bloke ruffling. Sophie felt herself blush and tried to concentrate as they perched on two large

51

rocks, munching their way through generous slices of Alice's cold lamb, boiled potatoes and salad. She poured out steaming tin mugs of tea from the thermos and offered Charlie a wedge of chocolate wattleseed cake.

He regarded her for a moment. 'You're an amazing person, Sophie,' he announced quietly. 'Obviously born to this life.'

She shrugged, humbly accepting his admiration. 'I grew up in the Western Australian outback, remember? It's in my blood.'

'All the same, only a certain calibre of woman has the strength of character to feel at home out here.' After a pause, he prompted, 'Tell me about your family.'

Here he was, wanting to get personal again. Good idea or trouble? Sophie sighed and relented. Charlie Kendall seemed genuine. Besides, she was finding him easier to talk to every time they met.

'I'm the oldest,' she began. 'My

brother Dusty runs the family wheat and sheep property, Sunday Plains. He married an Irish girl, Meghan, over a year ago now and they have a son, Benjamin, named after our great grandfather who settled the land. The last time I was home was for their wedding.' She smiled at the memory. 'My sister Sally married a neighbouring farmer, Phil Barnes. They have two kids. Oliver's at school now and they also have a baby daughter, Emily. They waited a long time for another child, so she's a special little blessing in their family. Your family's in Adelaide, you said,' she continued quickly before she realised how important family was to her and how much she missed them. She desperately tried to ignore the rising ache to create one of her own that hit her at odd moments these days.

Charlie reflected a moment, then said with reservation, 'My father Michael is a barrister. Could be thinking of retirement, but his profession is his life. My mother Anne is English. Her brother, my uncle Robert, inherited what is fondly known as the family pile, Westerfield Hall, in Norfolk. She loves socialising and does a lot of charity work. She loves her garden. To look at my mother, you wouldn't think she'd get her hands dirty.' Charlie grinned, a respectful degree of warmth in his voice. 'But she's pretty efficient at giving their gardener his orders.'

'What about your sister?'

'Amanda met her husband Warren through our father's legal practice in the city at some function or dinner, if I remember correctly.' His voice warmed with affection as he spoke. 'They have three kids. Jacob and Daniel are at school, and they also have little Charlotte. Dad and Warren work in partnership now. Warren will most likely assume the reins if Dad ever retires.'

'If you grew up in the city, how did you get interested in scratching around in the dirt?'

Charlie chuckled. 'Guess I can blame

my grandparents for that. Amanda and I spent most holidays down on their farm. I loved fossicking. Gramps faithfully kept all my finds in a big glass jar on a shelf in the sleep-out where I slept summer or winter. It was a closed-in veranda with timber shutters, no air conditioning or heating but a comfortable bed.'

Charlie's gaze wandered over the Ranges and Sophie suspected he was deep in nostalgia.

'You could see the sun or moon rising,' he continued, 'hear all the sounds of nature, smell the earth after rain. Didn't need much else.'

Sophie noted with a small degree of surprise that they shared a love of nature and the outdoors. She also realised they were both distanced to a certain degree from family, her own estrangement self-imposed since her father's death, escaping what she couldn't accept or change. Whereas Charlie's detachment seemed to have been thrust upon him at an early age.

She couldn't resist asking, 'You didn't miss your parents?'

He shrugged. 'They were busy people,' he said easily, denoting acceptance of his childhood. 'We got used to it and, honestly, I used to look forward to it,' he admitted, casting her an engaging devilish glance from behind the glasses. 'Our grandparents were loving people,' he said fondly.

'And your parents weren't?'

'Not demonstrably, no,' he admitted softly. 'But that's their way. I couldn't wait for the last day of term or semester to head for the farm. My grandmother's arms were always open the second we arrived, and somehow when I was smaller I always got lost in the folds of her big apron.' He chuckled. 'Gramps never said much. Didn't need to, I guess. Just sauntered along behind, his face creased into a grin, and we simply shook hands like men. I always valued that. He was a strong, quiet presence in our lives.'

'What did you do all day?'

'Amanda hung around the cottage and Grandmother's wild garden. They were always doing women's crafts together.' He smiled with affection. 'Probably where Amanda developed her love of interior decorating. But I'm afraid I disappeared for hours either on foot or clattering across the property tracks and paddocks on a battered old bicycle. Or I joined Gramps in his old Holden ute, checking stock. Helped him tend their huge vegetable garden and orchard. We all picked fruit in season that Amanda helped Gran transform into pies and preserves. I pretty much only returned to the cottage when I was hungry or it grew dark.'

'Sounds idyllic. There's something about living in the country, isn't there?'

'I live by the sea at West Beach at the moment,' Charlie revealed, 'but I haven't given up hope of a tree change one day. A few hectares of my own.'

'Really?' People often opted to move in the reverse direction, from the country to the coast. Sophie shouldn't have been surprised. She was discovering there was more country than city in this man. 'Then I hope you achieve it. It's a great life.'

'Out here you're fairly isolated. How do you handle a medical crisis, for example?'

She laughed. 'Hit the emergency button on the radio and get instructions from the RFDS.'

'Ever had to do that? Call the flying doctor?'

Sophie shook her head. 'Fortunately no. Only minor injuries so far, but living my whole life in the outback I've learned to be careful. Besides the radio, we have the satellite phone and wireless internet, so we can keep in touch.'

'I guess you need to stock up on things like food.'

'Yep. I put in my order by phone to the general store in town and they truck it out every month, or I'll take a trip in and do it myself. You need to keep your freezer full in case roads are impassable in winter, but that doesn't happen often out here with our limited rainfall. We're becoming quite civilised,' she mocked. 'These days much of the road is sealed, for which the locals and tourists are all grateful.' She heaved a loaded sigh. 'Just wish more of them swung our way. Jack doesn't think so, but after lean seasons we need them. Desperately. To pay the bills.'

'Like any landholder, you're at the mercy of nature,' Charlie observed knowingly.

Sophie nodded. 'Rain is erratic out here. We can get it any time of year. Monsoon storms from the north in summer might dump so much we flood. Not often, thankfully,' she ended, smiling.

Charlie squinted westward. 'Looks like clouds are building. Could be bad weather coming.'

Sophie grinned. 'We've learned not to get too excited until they actually drop rain, but you could be right.' Her gaze turned in the same direction.

'They're looking promising.' She kept a close eye on the forecast, but the sullen outback sky seemed more threatening than predicted. She voiced her concern just in case. 'If it's heavy while you're here, the water will run down the escarpments and swell the billabong and creeks. It won't flood your campsite, but it might get muddy and uncomfortable.'

Charlie shrugged philosophically. 'Working outdoors, we learn to live with it.'

'The water will head west out into the salt lakes. Lake Torrens has dozens of rivers and creeks flowing into it but it has only filled with water once in the last hundred and fifty years. Thunderstorms might turn the salt crust boggy, but it brings birds. It's a sight to behold when that happens. And noisy. Well, if we're done — ' Sophie stood up and dusted off the seat of her jeans. ' — we'll head on again.'

Charlie carried the hamper back to the ute. Along the way, in pockets of the landscape usually surrounded by the telltale remaining stands of trees, the isolated countryside occasionally revealed the ruins of an abandoned stone cottage — a relic from the past, like a graveyard of hopes.

'There are abandoned mines, too,' Sophie said. 'Cornishmen, mostly breaking their picks and their back and I suspect their hearts, in search of copper. We're isolated but there's a strong sense of community.'

They drove further around property tracks, slowing down at one point for a mob of emus to cross the road in single file in front of them. Closer in, large flocks of Casuarina Downs merinos contentedly grazed.

'Must be shearing soon,' Charlie commented knowledgeably.

'We're gradually bringing them in from all over the property on the quad bike with Drover's help. Jack musters them in the chopper from further out. The shearing contractors work solidly for over a month.'

'How much stock do you run?'

'We don't count the number of sheep per hectare in this country. You work out the amount of land needed to support one animal and keep it in good shape to hold them. Here on the Downs — ' Sophie shrugged as she drove along the track into the homestead block. ' — maybe one sheep for every four acres or one and a half hectares.'

'Not a lot.'

Sophie chuckled. 'Doesn't matter. Casuarina Downs is five hundred square kilometres. We have plenty of room.'

'Touché.' Charlie grinned and hesitated, something else clearly on his mind. 'I'd love to see more of your property if you have time.'

'Sure.' Sophie knew a buzz of warmth at his request, so she headed toward the homestead paddocks and pulled up in the outer yard. To the kelpie's delight, Sophie released Drover and he trotted around them as she and Charlie companionably explored together among the many outbuildings that always accompanied any substantial property, including the century-old native pine woolshed.

'What's in here?' Charlie used his shoulder to heave open the creaking timber door to a small stone building as they passed.

'We call it the workshop, but it's actually where we dump everything we find on the station. Old historic bits and pieces, mostly rusted. Jack won't throw anything away.'

'I'm not surprised. This is a serious man cave,' Charlie said eagerly, fighting his way through cobwebs and dust, stepping over relics on the floor. 'Plenty of people are fascinated by the past. All this stuff is interesting.'

Sophie shook her head, amused that anyone could be so excited over junk. 'If you say so.' She checked her watch, surprised to see it was already late afternoon. Charlie had proved to be easygoing and considerate by nature.

Time sped by in his company. He was also a gentleman. She had noticed it in little things: opening the ute door, looking behind if she followed as they walked and waiting for her to catch up. She sensed he continually watched out for her and felt respected in his presence.

'Jack not about today?' he asked as they shut and latched the workshop door.

'I thought he'd be in the woolshed starting to clean up for shearing, but maybe he's out around the sheep somewhere,' she said lightly.

After a moment of hesitation, Charlie regarded her closely and said quietly, 'He's fond of you.'

Sophie rubbed her arms self-consciously, surprised Charlie had picked up on Jack's attention. 'Yeah. We've been mates a long time and built up a special friendship.'

'His interest is understandable. You're an attractive, independent woman.'

'Thank you.' She felt herself blush. 'It's flattering of him, and he's a handsome man, but he's not for me.'

'Does *he* know that?'

Sophie frowned, irritated. 'I'm sure he does.'

All the same, Charlie's query prompted a degree of reservation in her mind. There had been the odd sign lately . . .

Sophie reflected whether it was wise to extend the invitation, and threw caution to the wind. 'If you can spare another half hour, I'm sure Alice has the kettle boiling.'

'How can I refuse?' he murmured in the rich mellow tone Sophie was, against her will and sensible reason, growing to treasure. 'It will finish off a memorable day in your charming company a while longer.'

'My pleasure to play host.' Sophie tried to act casual at the shameless warmth in his voice and steady, challenging gaze. Men rarely knocked her off her feet, but this one was certainly having a go. 'Stay,' Sophie told Drover under the veranda. The kelpie knew he was banned from the house but never failed to try sneaking in between legs if he could.

In the kitchen Alice was already pouring mugs of tea. 'What's for dinner?' Sophie perched on a stool at the kitchen island.

'Jack caught fish in the billabong.'

'He's around?'

Alice shook her head. 'Gone walk-about again.' She grinned.

So, he had decided to take the afternoon off as well. It might have been in spite, Sophie thought to herself in amusement. But whatever his reasons, she was pleased. He rarely relaxed and, despite her own initial misgivings, spending today with Charlie made her realise the importance of taking time out, too. She couldn't deny having enjoyed every moment in his company.

Alice produced hot pikelets dripping with butter and quandong jam, a peach-flavoured spread from the fruit of a native tree. 'What you think of Casuarina Downs, Mr. Charlie?' Alice asked as she poured milk into his tea.

Sophie wasn't surprised the cook remembered how he liked it. When Alice took to someone, they were unspoken friends for life. She called it their karma. Charlie had obviously breezed through her approval process.

He finished eating a pikelet and licked his fingers. 'It's extensive, and a credit to Sophie and Jack.'

Alice beamed, clearly pleased with his answer. 'My country is good country, all right.' To her there were no property boundaries, only the land to which she and her ancestors belonged.

Charlie fitted right in, Sophie marvelled. She had only seen him three times and spent mere hours in his company. Clearly he was highly educated and reserved, but beneath that cultivated exterior lay a man who rolled up his shirt sleeves and was every inch an equally rugged Australian man as any outback bloke she'd ever met.

Although she strongly rejected the possibility to herself, she found him attractive. After years of encountering tough suntanned men with their cheeky larrikin grins, it amazed her to find that a conservative, modest man like Charlie Kendall should be even remotely appealing to her.

Maybe because he reminded her of her brother Dusty, an outback gentleman. A lump filled her throat at thoughts of her family home in the west and another outback man — her father, Daniel. As a girl, she'd trailed him around Sunday Plains like a shadow. He taught her to ride, called her his offsider and showed her by example what a true and honest country man was. Unwanted emotions welled up in her at his memory, but she pushed them aside.

'Sophie?' Charlie was looking at her oddly.

'Yes?' she stared at him, unsettled.

'You were miles away.'

'Oh.' Uncomfortable at her lapse and

the direction her thoughts had taken, she said bluntly, 'I can take you back now,' and slid off the kitchen stool.

Charlie shrugged. 'Sure,' he said, adding to the cook with a glance over his shoulder, 'Thanks for the cuppa, Alice.'

Drover loyally waited at the door and when Sophie snapped her fingers and said, 'Let's go, fella,' he streaked across the yard and leapt into the back of the ute.

The return drive to the field camp was taken mostly in thoughtful silence. Another warm spring day was winding down and waterbirds had gathered on the billabong when they arrived. The site was silent and empty, Charlie's fellow campers still absent.

'Students are obviously enjoying their day off,' he commented. He opened the passenger door and swung his long legs out but glanced back at Sophie and laid a hand with gentle affection on her knee. 'Thanks for today. I appreciated it,' he said warmly.

'You're welcome,' was all she could say huskily.

Just a touch was unsettling. She hadn't felt this drawn toward any man in a long while. If ever. And she was terrified. Awareness flickered between them and for a fraction of a second, Sophie thought and almost hoped Charlie would make a move toward her. But his jaw clenched and, instead, he eased himself out. He shut the door and bent down to look in the open window.

'Guess we'll catch up again when we leave next week.'

'Yes.' Sophie leapt at an opportunity to break the personal pull that caused such strain and forced lightness into her voice to interrupt the charged atmosphere. 'The farewell barbeque.' She cringed at the thought of the group leaving when it seemed they had only just arrived. 'I'll radio later in the week to confirm times with you.'

'We should probably make it a lunch to give us time to get back to the city.'

'Of course.' She gunned the engine

and pulled away with a quick smile and wave. Drover barked, excited to be moving again.

Driving back to the homestead, Sophie felt a sense of loss she couldn't explain.

That evening she handed Jack his envelope of private mail. He looked uncomfortable as he accepted it, flashing a quick glance then looking away again. He hurriedly stuffed it into his shirt pocket with a muttered, 'Thanks.'

Sophie wondered why the station was in touch. She longed to know the contents but also knew it was none of her business. They had both lived and worked on Gulf River. Anyone from there could be approaching him for any number of reasons. But the unspoken mystery remained: *What was their reason for contacting Jack?*

* * *

Just when Sophie wanted the days of the following week to fly so she could see Charlie again, time dragged. Even working flat out, moving the last of the mobs of sheep with Jack and fighting the strong winds building daily, didn't dispel her impatience.

To her embarrassment, Jack noticed and remarked with blunt honesty, 'What's up with you?'

'Just be glad when mustering is done for another year,' she mumbled. She covered her confusion with a tight smile, flustered that her emotions were so obvious; annoyed that her resolve was so weak it showed. That she allowed herself to be so obsessed with any bloke. It hadn't been her style in recent years. Not since her father died suddenly, and especially not since her brother Dusty's first wife had been killed.

But unassuming Charlie Kendall had snuck under her radar and caught her unawares. At first she'd fought the crazy possibility; but since the tour around the property last Saturday, his charm had seeped into her heart and settled there. Damn it. The sooner he left, the better. Then she could be done and dusted with this girly crush and her life could return to its normal balance. Peaceful, uninterrupted, no threats to her emotional harmony.

She cast her contented gaze over the distant sweeping landscape. The property looked splendid in a good season like this, but it wasn't always tinged with green. Its beautiful red emptiness had won them both over, enough to gamble their future on taking over the pastoral lease for Casuarina Downs. Test the waters. See how she and Jack worked together as partners instead of as hired workers on someone else's station.

'Okay. Let's get back to work,' Sophie told Jack as she opened the next paddock gate to bring the sheep through.

Drover had been the cutest pup, and they'd been drawn to each other at first sight. With floppy ears that had pricked up later, he'd been adorably irresistible and grown into a handsome animal friend with a long, lean, athletic body. He was clever, hard-wired for stock work, and from the age of six months responded instinctively to all the commands of his training. These days he understood his task and circled back and forth at the rear and sides of the sheep.

Sophie whistled sharply. 'Come behind.' He crouched, watching, mouth open and panting.

With Jack in the distance herding the sheep toward them, Drover gathered the fragmented flock in the paddock and closed up the mob for moving. If a sheep grew nervous or startled and broke away, the kelpie quickly gathered it up and turned it back. Sophie was proud of her dog. He had a good eye, stalking the flock and holding them with just a gaze.

It wasn't long before they were done. Sophie met Jack back at the gate as he drove through and she closed it behind him. They chatted while he tried to light a cigarette, cupping his hand around the match against the gusty breeze.

'It's going to be good year,' she said.

'Yep, for sure.'

Sophie edged closer to him as they hung over the gate and companionably rubbed shoulders. 'Any chance of taking our guests up in the chopper?'

'Don't have time at the moment. Besides, it's too windy.'

Sophie sighed. 'My biggest regret is not learning to fly when I had the chance. It's on my bucket list. You're coming for the farewell barbeque next week, aren't you?'

He shrugged. 'Probably.'

'I thought one of those cute young women in the group might interest you,' she teased.

He slid her a long, soft glance. 'You know I'm not looking.'

That was what she was afraid of. Judging by his gentle tone when he spoke, Sophie agonised that in Jack's mind their mateship might mean more.

She had to set him straight.

'Jack,' she warned with a groan, then pushed herself away from the gate. She laid a hand gently on his arm. 'Try and get your own life, Jack. Please.'

'Bit hard out here,' he snapped.

'Then take a few days off,' she suggested. 'Go down to Adelaide.' He darted her a black glare. 'Okay, maybe not the city. There's plenty of coast further south. Alice and I can cope, and shearing is still a month away.' When he hesitated, she begged softly, 'At least promise me you'll think about it.'

He dismissed her plea with a careless shrug.

Frustrated, she whistled for Drover. 'I'm heading back to the house. You in for dinner tonight? Alice is cooking lamb,' she laughed.

'What else would it be?' He grinned, and for now their disharmony seemed repaired.

* * *

At dinner that night, as thunder rumbled and it was clear the weather was closing in, Alice only made things worse over Jack's emerging fondness for Sophie.

'Those rock people sure got good appetites,' she said as they all sat around the dining table replete after their meal.

Sophie was finishing a glass of Barossa Valley chardonnay and Jack nursed one of many beers he'd had tonight.

'That was your good cooking, Alice.'

'You and that Charlie fella do good talking.' She grinned widely, exposing her crooked teeth.

Jack glowered. 'Found yourself a new mate?'

Sophie was horrified he should be so sensitive to any mention of Charlie. 'He's our guest,' she protested.

'I thought you were *my* mate,' he growled.

'Always will be.' Sophie tried to keep the conversation light to lessen the strain. Honestly, this couldn't go on. They were overdue for a heart-to-heart and it wouldn't be easy for either of them. She pushed back her chair and rose. 'Alice, let's attack the dishes, then I suggest we all turn in.'

Jack reluctantly followed her lead, bid goodnight and strode off to the cottage. When the women had tidied up, Sophie took a mug of coffee outside and leant against a veranda post, mulling over Jack's unfortunate affection.

'Don't worry about him, missus,' Alice said, approaching quietly. 'He get over it.'

'He's a handsome, charming bloke,' Sophie sighed, warily eyeing the brewing storm. 'He helped me when I first started as a jillaroo. We struck up an easy friendship and worked on stations together, but I've only ever thought of him like a brother. A good mate. Lately, he's wearing his heart on his sleeve, Alice. But he's going to have to give it to someone else.' Her voice caught with emotion and she almost laughed at the irony of two men in her life at the moment where usually there were none. And her instinct to push them both away. Each for a different reason.

'He find his own woman. Take time.'

'He's a loner who needs his space; but because of his childhood, he deliberately holds himself apart. If he just found someone who loved him fiercely and wouldn't go away, it would make him stop and think. Maybe he would be unable to resist.'

'I shouldn't say this, missus, but he don't belong here.'

'Oh Alice, bite your tongue,' Sophie gasped.

She shrugged and said simply, 'He belongs Malak Malak country where he grew up.'

'You think so?' Sophie regarded Alice with respect. Her indigenous background endowed her with a certain intuitive wisdom that often proved true. 'Up on the Daly River in the Territory?'

Alice nodded. 'He not my people, but he born there, so maybe he belong up there, eh? Maybe he go back one day.'

Sophie knew Aboriginal people had a strong spiritual feeling for the countryside. Land was fundamental to them but wasn't owned. Everyone belonged to a certain territory and had connections and obligations to it. So she was horrified to hear Alice's predictions and hoped if Jack ever decided to leave, that the time would be in the distant future. For now, they had the Casuarina Downs leasehold to build up together.

'Who are your people, Alice?' Sophie sipped her coffee. She had never thought to ask before.

Alice produced a rare and playful grin. 'Adnyamathanha.'

Sophie spluttered on her drink and laughed. 'That's a mouthful.'

'Means hill people.' Alice's black face beamed with pride and she spread out the fingers of one hand. 'Five tribes in our traditional group of the Ranges and Lake Torrens.'

Sophie knew Alice shared a common bond of language and culture from her ancestors. She reflected on where her own place was meant to be. Although she had been born over in the west, she loved it out here. The peace. The stark beauty. And she was shocked to begin feeling the need for that special someone in her life. An image of a bespectacled charismatic geologist flashed into her mind but she ignored it.

* * *

Later that evening, steady rain began drumming on the homestead's iron roof and settled in for the night. Sophie's thoughts, after what an extra boost it would be for the sheep pastures, was concern for the campers. She considered taking a run down to the billabong to ensure everything was okay, but hesitated. Hadn't Charlie said geologists learned to live with the weather? They certainly wouldn't be achieving much tomorrow.

Next morning, even though the rain

had eased, it continued all day. Mid-afternoon, the radio crackled into life and Sophie sprinted into her office. Charlie's deep, warm voice advised her the geologists had broken camp and would stop by the homestead before returning to Adelaide. Sophie's shoulders sagged at the regrettable news and she was swamped with a sense of guilt over the unseasonal soggy deluge, although it was hardly her fault and there was nothing anyone could do about it.

Within half an hour they appeared. The sodden huddle of students remained in the vehicles as Charlie dashed across the yard in the rain to meet Sophie waiting under the shelter of the veranda.

'I would apologise for this — ' She nodded toward the steady torrent pouring down and pulled a wry smile. ' — but we never refuse it.'

'Nothing anyone can do,' he said generously, with a philosophical shrug. He removed his rain-spattered glasses and produced a huge handkerchief to wipe them. 'Just wanted to acknowledge and thank you for your hospitality. The location and work were fabulous this past week. With your permission, I'll recommend future camps to the university.' He studied her hopefully as he replaced his glasses.

She really shouldn't give it without Jack's approval. It would be easy enough to dash across to the cottage, but instead she said eagerly, 'Absolutely. I'd appreciate it.' She wondered if Charlie would return to lead them.

'Wonderful. We had a most productive trip,' he enthused, his warm brown eyes gleaming over her. 'But I didn't want to push the girls on their first foray out into the field. They were being brave but, as happy and fit as they are, a couple of them were flagging. So on behalf of myself and the whole gang, thanks again.'

'My pleasure,' she murmured, and meant it. 'Should I contact the university for a partial refund for your interrupted camp?' she offered, though knowing the outward cash flow would be unfortunate.

'I wouldn't bother,' he drawled, his mouth tweaking into an easy grin. 'I'd say we all got value for money this week.'

He hesitated, making no move to leave, and placed a hand at her elbow. With those seductive eyes settled on her face, Sophie knew she was in deep trouble. Charlie's loaded comment and that intent gaze only confirmed a mutual unspoken interest, and her heart wouldn't behave. He said simply, 'I'd like to keep in touch.'

Sophie swallowed. 'Um . . . ' All kinds of alarms rang in her head.

Charlie frowned and cleared his throat. 'Have I read you wrong?'

Daunted by the urge to be nothing but honest with this gorgeous, humble man, Sophie was forced to shake her head and admit quietly, 'No.'

In the past, she would never have allowed herself an interest in any man, nor would he have received a second glance, no matter how enticing and attractive.

He sighed and moved closer. 'That's a relief.' He handed her a business card. 'Has my email and phone numbers. No pressure.' He smiled gently.

Self-conscious, Sophie tucked it into the back pocket of her jeans. 'You should get going,' she prompted with forced brightness, cringing that she sounded unfriendly, so she tempered her irreversible words by adding, 'You have a long, dismal drive home.'

Charlie smiled softly and shook her hand. While he still held it, he pulled her closer into a brief hug and brushed a passing tender kiss on her cheek as they broke apart again. Sophie vaguely heard some whistles from the students inside the van and felt herself blush.

Just to add to her embarrassment, at that exact moment Jack, with little else to do on such a wet day, yet having taken little interest in their paying guests all week, emerged under the homestead veranda and saw the kiss, too. She caught his dark gaze over Charlie's shoulder.

Unaware of Jack behind him, Charlie winked and murmured, 'A pleasure meeting you, Sophie Nash. I'll be in touch.'

The promise lifted her heart. 'Safe travels.'

He shrugged his coat collar higher and dashed back out into the rain to his four-wheel drive as Jack appeared and stood alongside her, brooding with disapproval.

She waved them goodbye, feeling a twinge of loss at Charlie's departure and waves of tension from her mate alongside. She drew in a long, deep breath and her heart ached for what she knew she must do.

'You looked cosy with Kendall,' Jack challenged, his comment tinged with envy.

'It was just a friendly hug,' she protested. 'Not a passionate embrace.' Needing to implant a hint of what was to follow, she decided to champion Charlie and lightly tease him. 'He's a good bloke, which you would have discovered yourself if you'd bothered to get to know him while he was here. Or anyone for that matter.' She tempered her disapproval with a nudge and a grin.

Jack had the grace to look mildly sheepish. His dark hair and equally dark flashing eyes, deep tan that barely faded over winter, and brooding personality made him a chick magnet. If only he realised it. Everyone but the man himself could see he needed a woman. The sad part was, as much as Sophie might wish it otherwise, it could never be her.

Suffering mixed emotions of a sunny private glow from Charlie's unexpectedly warm farewell hug and kiss, and anxiety at Jack's rebuke over the attention, Sophie knew it was time for action. With the vehicles now out of sight, she turned resignedly to him. 'Can I come see you at the cottage in fifteen?'

Jack scowled, wise to the reason perhaps. He nodded curtly and disappeared. Sensitive over her new feelings for Charlie, Sophie didn't need Jack's added resentment, even though she knew why and sympathised. Admitting to any attraction for a man was a big step for her. A little support would have been appreciated instead.

Sophie untied Drover and took a calming stroll around the homestead block. The heavy cloudbank was slowly moving on, but the grey sky matched her mood. Spring rains were rare and the extra feed they generated always welcome.

Sophie watched the winds toss the flimsy tops of gum trees. Thoughts of Charlie only brought confusion into her mind, and her attraction for him became a challenging disruption to her settled life. She wasn't sure she was ready for whatever developments might unfold since Charlie had expressed his wish to keep in touch.

She regarded the homestead from a distance; it sat solidly at the centre of the property with always the purple and green Ranges beyond, looking just like the countless transparent watercolour paintings that artists captured of the distinctive outback landscape.

Taking a deep breath against the coming encounter with Jack, Sophie walked toward his stone cottage, his scuffed boots on the step as usual. She knocked. He opened it without a word and stepped back into the room. She entered and closed the door behind her.

She sank her hands into her jeans pockets and leaned against a wall. 'You promised, Jack.' She sighed softly with frustration and turned a level gaze on him. 'We had this conversation three years ago before we took up the Casuarina Downs lease.'

Smoke lingered around him and he shuffled. 'I admit, it's hard watching you with another man.'

'Then you lied, didn't you? You promised me buying this property together was strictly business. You assured me you didn't want to be in on the partnership just to be with me. Sure, we had a spark of attraction early on in our friendship, but it was over long ago. I've never led you on.' Sophie rose and paced before the hearth, rubbing her arms. 'You know, I doubted your word even back then, but I wanted this property so badly I forced myself to believe you. Trusted you to be honest with me and ignored my intuition.'

'Okay,' he muttered impatiently. 'So I'm only here to be with you,' he reluctantly confessed.

Sophie cringed. Exactly what she feared. 'I wish you weren't. Now look where we are.' She reached out and rested a hand gently on his arm, swallowing back tears. 'I feel so bad I can't love you back like you want me to, Jack,' she whispered. 'But I can tell you now, next to my father, you're the best friend and mate I've ever had. Tell me that won't change,' she pleaded.

They stared at each other, then

reached out for a fierce hug of mutual comfort as friends.

'Promise.' She barely heard his vow.

Sophie pulled away and shrugged. 'Look, I don't know where my friendship with Charlie will lead. Honestly,' she confided. 'For now I'll just accept it for what it is. An attraction. It'll probably blow over.' She voiced her hopes only because the alternative scared the jeans off her backside.

'From what I saw,' Jack mumbled, 'that isn't likely to happen.'

They both saw the irony and grinned, each wishing it were otherwise, but for vastly different reasons. As fate would have it, Sophie reflected in amazement, she who never deliberately sought out any man, nor allowed herself to respond to any attraction before, now had two handsome charismatic men in pursuit. One cheeky and restless, whom she'd known for years. The other deeper, but with a quietly charming sense of humour, who had only recently stumbled across her life's path.

'Charlie's gone back to the city. I might never see him again,' she protested weakly, feeling like a traitor for saying it when her feelings so strongly dictated otherwise and he had promised to keep in touch. But would he?

'He's keen on you. He'll be back,' Jack grumbled. After a hesitation, he cleared his throat. 'Truth is, I'm not sure I can stick around and watch you with some other bloke.'

Sophie gasped, not wanting to believe him, but sensing so much underlying pain in his remark, her heart ached for him. 'Jack, you're not serious? You'd leave?'

He butted out his cigarette in the ashtray and nodded, sitting forward, his hands folded between his knees. He didn't look at her as he spoke. 'If it doesn't happen with Charlie, some other bloke will come along. You came here to settle down. You said it yourself. You wanted to put down roots. Fact is,' he added, pushing a restless hand through his hair, 'as much as I care about you, I'm not sure I do. Yet.'

'You'll change when the right woman happens along.'

If her own personal experience lately was any indication, it would be when he least expected it. Like her, would he fight it and struggle, too?

'We have quite a history, don't we, Jack?' She stared into the cold fireplace and sank into a decade of memories. 'After I left home following my father's sudden death and headed to outback stations in the Territory, remember?'

He nodded. Ten years ago they'd grown together, each needing the other on their journey to healing. Jack from his tough childhood, Sophie from so abruptly losing the person she loved most in the world and with whom she had shared a close and special bond. It hadn't mattered to Daniel Nash that his firstborn was female; they had simply clicked. The father had idealised his laughing blonde-haired daughter. Sophie's world collapsed when he died. Even now a lump formed in her throat, her heart ached with his loss, and her eyes misted in nostalgia.

'Look at me. Ten years on and I'm still soppy.' She wiped her damp eyes.

Jack knew her past and exactly what she meant. He reached for her hand and squeezed it. 'I guess you never forget those you love.'

Sophie heard the sorrow and regret in his voice, perhaps because growing up he had never experienced the same. And now, through no fault of her own, she couldn't return the love he wanted and perhaps desperately needed in his life.

'Orphans can have families, too,' she pointed out gently. 'But you have to go out and find them.'

'I thought I had,' he said wryly, his injured expression softening her heart.

Her spirits sank under the weight of running Casuarina Downs alone. 'You won't change your mind?' He shook his head. 'When are you thinking of going?' she dared to ask.

'I'll keep my stake in the place until you find another partner.' He winced as he said it and they both knew what he meant.

Sophie's shoulders sagged in relief. 'Great.'

'I'd never bolt and leave you stranded.'

'I know. Thanks. I appreciate it.'

'As soon as you find another regular man, jackeroo or whatever, and we run him in, I'll leave.'

She could see by the stiff set of his stubbled jaw he was trying hard to be outwardly strong. Physically he could ride all day in the saddle or rope and pin down any steer. She knew because she'd ridden alongside him and seen him do it. Emotions were a different story. He'd never known the love and stability of a true family home. Just a series of kind families who'd taken him in but mainly used him as labour.

'Where will you go?'

'Head back to the Territory. Got plenty of contacts up there.'

Sophie reflected with irony on Alice's prediction that she sensed Jack wasn't meant to live here.

'You know me. I'm just as happy working for someone else,' Jack said, pausing. 'Have a confession to make. You saw my mail from Gulf River?'

Sophie nodded and, in the light of their conversation, the penny dropped.

'I only contacted them on the off chance,' he said hastily.

'No need for explanations.'

'I know we've always been up front with each other, so I felt bad going behind your back. Just sounding them out.'

'And?' She raised her eyebrows, grinning. She could guess the outcome.

'They'll hire me for next season from the end of the wet.'

'It's great up there.' She tried to sound excited for him. 'March or April, then?'

He nodded. That gave her a few

months' grace to recruit new workers, but it still left the dilemma of finding another financial backer or partner, silent or active. Where could she find one? And it would take more than one full tourist season, even with dual incomes for the station accounts, to look healthy enough before she would rest easy that Casuarina Downs was in a stable economic position.

Walking across the yard from Jack's cottage back to the homestead a short time later as raindrops fell, running down Sophie's face like tears and dampening her shirt and hair, she barely noticed but absently thought it appropriate that the weather should reflect her mood. Instead, she forced herself to stay positive and focus on replacing Jack. They'd been such a team over the years, it hardly seemed possible they would be splitting up and going their separate ways.

Sophie faced the strange situation of finding someone else compatible to live and work alongside. A challenge, but after consideration, she debated Jack's suggestion of hiring a jackeroo. Why couldn't a right-hand man be a right-hand woman? Why not make Casuarina Downs a female outfit? She'd bet there were plenty of young women out there seeking an opportunity to get onto the land. Sophie had been in the same situation ten years ago. If it hadn't been for that first station owner giving her a break, she wouldn't be running her own property today.

But when she settled in front of her laptop in the office later with a mug of tea to research outback recruitment websites, her gaze drifted out the window at the dismal rain-washed yard and her thoughts centred on Charlie and his company driving back to Adelaide in the downpour. They wouldn't make the city until after dark.

* * *

Within a day, the sudden spring weather front passed and the clouds scooted away, pushed by a frisky wind, and the sun even tried to shine again.

Over the following weeks, before shearing began and moved into full swing — their busiest time of year — Sophie sent out feelers and advertised for a jillaroo on Casuarina Downs. Emails flooded her inbox. She sifted through them, reading between the lines and setting up Skype interviews with those who looked most likely.

One young woman in particular caught her attention. During their online conversation, Sophie grinned to herself, impressed by the short cropped hair, the bouncy confidence, plus the twinkle in her eye and sparkly personality. All round she seemed to have the goods Sophie sought.

So she invited her out to the property for a firsthand assessment. When the bubbly redhead drove up to the homestead three days later in a battered but clearly beloved ancient blue ute with a beautiful border collie named Harley safely chained in the back,

Sophie was sold.

She strode out to meet her in the yard, noting the strong handshake and all-black outfit: jeans, polo shirt, boots and wide-brimmed hat. This was a girl from the bush, born and bred.

'Hi, I'm Sophie Nash. Welcome to Casuarina Downs.'

'Ms Nash,' she acknowledged. 'Billie Smith. Great place.' She looked around eagerly.

'Let's walk, and bring your dog.'

Billie beamed and untied him. They bypassed the house and strolled the homestead block and adjoining paddock as they talked.

'Tell me all about yourself, Billie, and why you want to work out here.'

She grinned and shrugged. 'I grew up in a small country town. My parents were drovers and carted us three kids along. I loved it and learned to ride soon after I walked, so I'm told. Drove paddock bashers with my brothers when we stayed put long enough and Dad was around to help build them.

100

Mum did the home schooling thing for a few years, then my folks decided to settle. Give us kids a shot at an education. Civilisation made me tough. Billie's short for hillbilly,' she chuckled. 'Kids at school thought I was a country bumpkin. Real name's Alexandra, but don't tell anyone or I'll have to rope and gag you.'

Sophie threw back her head and laughed.

'I've grown used to Billie,' the newcomer said.

Sophie admired her resilience. It showed strength of character, and her arrival was like a breath of fresh air around the place. 'Parents still alive?'

'Yep. They work a smallholding down south on the coast. Us kids are all independent now, but they head out on the droving trail still sometimes to keep in practice. They just love the outdoors. Rubbed off on all of us.' She smiled fondly.

Sophie heard the warmth in her voice and knew, despite her nomadic lifestyle, she hailed from a close family. As a result, she seemed stable and reliable. Billie was starting to tick some boxes.

'I've had plenty of experience. Promise I'll work hard,' she emphasised.

'I've read your application,' Sophie said. 'Impressive. You haven't let grass grow under your feet.'

'They haven't been still long enough,' she joked. 'Apart from being a jillaroo since my late teens, I started at an agricultural college, but I couldn't stick it. I needed more action and hands-on work. By seventeen I was over classrooms.'

'Well, it's paid off. Your practical grounding is excellent and just what we're seeking.' She turned in the direction of Jack's cottage. 'There's someone I want you to meet.'

Sophie knocked on his door. Knowing Billie was coming today, she'd asked him to hang around. When he emerged, Sophie introduced him. 'My partner on Casuarina Downs, Jack Bryce.'

Billie whistled softly. 'Life's looking up around here. Pleased to meet you, Mr. Bryce.'

Jack blushed beneath his tan. Sophie stifled her amusement and stopped herself from gaping at Billie's boldness. He may have met his match in this energetic young thing.

Later, while Alice entertained Billie in the kitchen, Sophie and Jack held an impromptu conference in the office.

'She's ideal,' Sophie enthused.

'Didn't expect a woman, but I'll go along with your judgement,' Jack said with a shrug, playing down his own fascination. 'You have to work with her.'

'So do you for the coming months. You'll be helping me show her the ropes.'

They returned to the kitchen. 'Billie,' Sophie announced, 'you've got yourself a job.'

'Yahoo!' She beamed, sliding off the stool to vigorously shake hands with them both. 'Thank you, ma'am. Mr. Bryce.'

'From now on, it's Sophie and Jack,' her new boss said.

And so jillaroo Billie Smith entered their lives.

★ ★ ★

In the preoccupation of hiring a new full-time worker and processing Jack's bombshell of leaving Casuarina Downs, Sophie had little time to dwell on Dr. Charlie Kendall, but he hovered in her subconscious all the time.

Then shearing approached, and the three of them cleaned out the woolshed and shearers' quarters before the team of seasonal men arrived. Billie shadowed Jack wherever he went. She claimed it was to learn as much from him as she could before he left. Sophie wasn't the least envious, because Jack was her senior by some years and possessed greater overall experience. The jillaroo's devotion reminded Sophie of Drover as a pup when he scampered playfully underfoot while she raised and trained him.

When the phone rang one evening while they were all seated around the table during dinner, Sophie set down her knife and fork and rose to answer it. 'I'll take it in the study.'

Distracted by dinner conversation that had centred on shearing and all of its trappings to be organised, she snatched up the handset. 'Casuarina Downs. This is Sophie.'

'Evening. Nice to hear your voice again.'

She didn't need to ask the caller's identity. She'd recognise that deep, expressive voice anywhere. Sophie dropped down into the office chair and her heart skipped a beat. 'Charlie.'

'Didn't think I'd call?' he quipped over the silence while she sat tongue-tied, clinging to the phone.

'No,' she breathed. 'No. I'm pleased you did.' He hadn't forgotten her!

'Sorry it's been a few weeks. I compiled an extensive report of the field camp. The university science department was so impressed they have approved funding for more trips.'

He was coming back, presuming he led future camps. And they would have extra income after all. It wouldn't be much but it was a start. She barely concentrated while he continued.

'I've roughed out some ideas and dates. I'm thinking four a year in each term and semester break. When would it suit to meet and discuss the schedule? I could come out to Casuarina Downs any weekend,' he suggested when she remained silent.

Sophie sighed. She would love nothing more. 'Lovely idea but lousy timing. We're about to start shearing and that usually goes on for four to five weeks.' She hoped he didn't think she was turning him away or that she didn't want to see him and wasn't interested. Hearing his voice again and knowing he'd been thinking of her, too, only fanned the flame of attraction.

Her fears vanished when he said softly, 'Not sure I can wait that long.

Guess I'll have to email it to you then.'
He sounded disappointed.

He could have done that anyway.
'Sorry. Best I can do at the moment,'
she apologised and gave him her email
address. 'By the end of each shearing
day I'm usually fairly weary. I wouldn't
be much company anyway. Probably
fall asleep,' she explained.

'Fair enough,' he chuckled, and she
cherished the deep, warm sound. 'I'm
not interrupting anything? Do you have
time to talk?'

Sophie thought of her dinner growing
cold. 'Absolutely.'

'How's everything out there?'

Sophie sank back into her office
chair, more pleased than she cared to
admit that he seemed in no rush to
hang up and wanted to prolong the
conversation. 'It's all go before shearing, of course. The men are starting to
arrive.' She felt comfortable talking to
him and updated him on recent
changes. 'Jack's leaving.'

'Really?'

'I believe he would have moved on again eventually anyway. He's still restless.'

'How do you feel about his decision?'

'I'll miss him,' she admitted cautiously, 'but we're both in different places in our lives right now. He wants to head back up north.'

'Where does that leave you and Casuarina Downs?'

Sophie sighed. 'Shy of a business partner and short-handed. I've hired a young jillaroo, Billie.' She laughed. 'She stalks Jack and he pretends to mind but he's secretly flattered. She's a hard worker and she'll learn heaps from him. Enough about me. How's Adelaide?'

'Busy. Noisy.' She caught a note of regret in his voice. 'I've been thinking about your station. You have huge scope to value-add even more tourism dollars,' he went on.

'My thoughts exactly. I don't like to say it, but without Jack's resistance, it leaves me open to explore every avenue possible,' she said eagerly, her spirits lifting to share her ideas and plans. She appreciated the sounding board. Charlie's interest was unexpected, reinforcing her instincts that tourism was the route she must take.

'Can you see yourself sharing your outback paradise with the world?' he asked.

She loved his accolade of her home. Some people only saw a harsh landscape hours from civilisation. 'An unnerving thought, but yes.'

'The field camps are a start. You've already dipped your toes into the water there. Plus I noticed that the day we toured around, you have bags of untapped accommodation on the property for starters. The existing cottages and shearers' wing could be renovated and upgraded. Whitewashed, rugs on the floor, basic furniture. The partial ruins further out could be rebuilt. Make great little studio B&Bs.'

'That *would* be a project.' She frowned, trying not to sound too cautious, amazed that Charlie had given her options so much thought in his absence. She hadn't even thought that far ahead herself yet. Even if it were feasible, there was the small matter of cash to finance it all.

'But it's doable,' Charlie said encouragingly. 'I suspect most of the stone slabs are still among the rubble. A stonemason could easily restore them in a few months.'

Sophie tried to imagine them finished, lined inside, each with a cosy open fireplace. Maybe a kitchenette in one corner and a bathroom behind a screen in another.

'Their rustic simplicity would be their attraction.' Charlie took the thought from her mind.

'You make it all sound so easy,' she sighed. 'It would take work.' And money that she didn't have. The future of her property was becoming exciting and daunting at the same time. Not to mention the cost and labour involved to achieve it, and determination to carry it through.

'Break it down into manageable projects. Most important stuff first. You could start with what you've already got — the homestead.'

Whereas Sophie had always coasted along knowing Jack's apathy toward tourism, she could see Charlie had an organised mind. Not to mention a natural brimming enthusiasm.

'It's huge and half-empty,' she admitted. 'We only use the kitchen and living areas and two of the six bedrooms.'

She considered the potential. Other properties in the region had converted their lovely big bedrooms into suites of top-notch accommodation. At some places, the owners flew people in and out on charters.

Charlie must have sensed her reservations. 'It's a big ask to open up your own home to others,' he said gently. 'Maybe it's something to consider at a later date after you've seen how your other ventures go.' He changed the subject. 'You know that old workshop you showed me?'

She chuckled. 'You're being tactful and generous. It's a junk room and we know it.'

'People will stumble over themselves to look at fascinating old relics. You could set it up as a museum. You might even consider selling the excess, paring its contents down to the essentials. Don't charge an entry fee but maybe set up a donation box by the door. Most folks would drop in a gold coin donation.'

'It would all mount up and I could easily produce information labels for the displays.' Sophie visualised the workshop's potential. At the moment, it was a treasure trove waiting to be unlocked and revealed.

'There are countless other groups besides geologists and archaeologists that would love access to your corner of that striking landscape. Photographers, artists. Albert Namatjira and Hans Heysen would be the most famous, who have so beautifully portrayed the region in paintings.'

'True.' Her mind buzzed with excitement at the scope of potential. 'Thank you for your encouragement. You're an inspiration.'

'You're welcome. I know you can do it.'

Sophie considered the difference between Jack's restraint and Charlie's passion. She sensed life on Casuarina Downs was about to enter a whole new phase. Charlie's suggestions all had merit. She would investigate after shearing. Instead of feeling overwhelmed at tackling the project on her own, she now burst with eagerness to begin.

'Thought it might be worth mentioning,' Charlie went on. 'My sister Amanda is an interior designer and my mother has an influential social circle. I can run it by them first and if you're agreeable and can get down to Adelaide, I'm sure they'd help. Amanda will have bags of ideas and know the best suppliers and dealers.

Her input especially would be valuable.'

'That's an extremely generous offer.' Sophie's mouth dropped open. 'It would be a fabulous opportunity — but your family don't know me.'

'Can't hurt to ask them and use their connections and expertise. I'll let you know.'

Sophie examined the prospect of being drawn into Charlie's family. She knew he would pursue their relationship with the slightest encouragement.

The last thing she wanted was to hurt him, but ten years ago she made a promise about involvement. With that in mind, should she end it now? Not take any more phone calls? Keep him at bay? She certainly had an excuse. Shearing was about to start. But the bottom line was, she didn't have the heart to do it. More surprising still, she discovered she didn't want to.

She found herself wistful when they said good night and hung up. Most unlike her usual resilience, but Dr.

Kendall was proving hard to resist. Sophie stared out the window as dusk settled its blue-grey shadows over everything. Was this longing, this pull, what a man and woman felt when it was the real thing? Had her parents felt it? Her brother Dusty and his wife Meghan? She could only imagine how devastating it must be losing that other special person in your life. Her mother had never been quite the same after her father died, and it had taken Dusty years to gather the courage to marry again after his first wife was killed.

When Sophie returned to the kitchen, she still felt alive from her chat with Charlie. All eyes swung in her direction and gaped. She touched her cheek. Was she flushed?

Alice bustled over to the oven and brought her half-eaten dinner back to the table. 'Kept it hot for you.'

'Everything all right?' Jack stared.

Sophie didn't intend to be secretive about Charlie's phone call, but to spare Jack's raw feelings she said simply, 'Just some post-shearing organisation.' She brushed it off to discourage any further comment on the subject. Not too far off the truth.

Although Jack would still be around for a few months, Sophie didn't want to mention or emphasise the fact that she had tourism plans underway even before his booted feet were out the door. Her strategy would only come into play after he was gone, so it seemed pointless to raise it. Meanwhile, shearing was their priority. Expansion would have to wait.

As Jack left later, Sophie pulled him aside. 'How's it going supervising Billie?'

'She won't leave me out of her sight,' he grumbled.

'You're her idol. She's keen to learn. You should be flattered,' she teased.

★　★　★

Although wool was the backbone of the income on Casuarina Downs, Sophie was itchy for shearing to finish. The region experienced an excellent season with a high percentage of lambs to strengthen future flocks.

What bothered her was the fact that Charlie didn't phone or send a follow-up email as promised. Unlike him. He was usually trustworthy. Had she offended him by putting him off? Yet their long telephone conversation has been heartening.

Secretly anxious, she didn't know whether his lack of communication was a blessing or a concern. She could have contacted him and, a few times, her hand actually hovered over the phone. But she never actually picked it up as her old demons resurfaced.

Meanwhile Jack, Billie, she and Alice all threw themselves into the annual frenzy that was shearing. Along with the kitchen girl, Niley, also from the local indigenous community and whom they always hired at this hectic time of year, Alice in her usual measured way coped with meals and rose before daylight organising a full breakfast delivered over to the shearers' quarters.

Jack only emerged when Billie pounded on his cottage door and yelled, 'Grub's up, Tiger,' for everyone to hear.

Sophie just shook her head and grinned. She swore the jillaroo did it on purpose to deliberately bait Jack and draw him out more. His unsociable manner didn't bother the girl. In fact, she seemed to consider him a challenge. Sophie watched the unfolding process with amusement, silently wishing Billie luck with her endeavours.

As if by instinct, Charlie finally phoned the day after shearing cut out. Sophie relaxed at the sound of his voice when she should have been on her guard. Somehow amid the forthcoming changes on Casuarina Downs he had become her invisible anchor, and she suspected he had deliberately waited until now to make contact.

Naturally, talk turned to tourism again and with shearing over for another year, Sophie could devote more attention. When they had been chatting for a while, Sophie said eagerly, 'Alice suggested guided Aboriginal tours to ancestral rock-painting and sacred sites on the property. I'm ashamed to admit I didn't think of the traditional landowners' aspect myself.'

'Brilliant idea. She's a treasure.'

'She knows the right people and elders in her community. I've asked her to approach them and sound them out. She felt they might be reluctant or protective.'

'Well from my end, Amanda's intrigued by your plans, and it won't take Mother more than a few phone calls to arrange meetings with her friends to gauge interest in art weekends and collect some propositions.'

'Great.' Sophie leaned back in her office chair and put her feet up on the desk.

'So when can you come down to Adelaide for a few days for discussions over dinner with the womenfolk? Amanda said to bring pictures of what you want; the kind of decor you have in mind for accommodation. Later on if you decide to collaborate, you can give her a list of exactly what you need and a budget and she'll source it for you. She has a stable of contacts and dealers.'

Sophie felt daunted and hesitant about the visit, but her tourism plans were too important. She must swallow her misgivings and accept all the help and advice she could get. Still, being pressed for a decision threw her into chaos. Clearly he meant sooner rather than later. Before Christmas. She would see Charlie again. But she shouldn't. She should refuse. For a grown woman to feel so undecided was ridiculous, but she'd always kept men at arm's length.

Sophie drew in a deep breath. 'Weekend after next?'

'Perfect.'

She heard the smile in his voice and wondered with more than a small amount of misgiving what on earth she was getting herself into.

* * *

Sophie calculated that if she started early enough Saturday morning and returned late Sunday night, she could manage the lengthy hours of driving without having to stay any longer in Adelaide than necessary. She hated traffic and noise. Besides, less contact with Charlie might be wise, and she was determined to keep the weekend professional.

She left the homestead before daylight and expected to arrive in the city by midday. She had arranged to meet Charlie on North Terrace, one of the four main streets bounding the central capital in a square, since it was the location of his university campus. Sophie was to park her ute in the grounds then he would drive her out to the hills where his parents lived.

The swell of bustle, bumper-to-bumper traffic, and general rushing about assaulted her senses, which were usually more attuned to wind, the open outback sky above, and peaceful isolation. How did people live in such a noisy mess? She slowed the ute along the Terrace. Uncertainty and butterflies kicked into play when she caught sight of Charlie, the first time for almost two months.

He leant against his four-wheel drive, legs and arms casually crossed. His face broke into a smile as he straightened and strode toward the ute, jiggling his keys, when Sophie pulled up alongside.

With one sweeping glance, he took in everything about her. He opened the door. 'You're worth the wait.'

Easy. Sophie took a deep breath for composure. Hard to be casual when he was so close. 'Am I late?'

'No,' he chuckled. 'I'm just impatient.'

Alighting from the ute, Sophie stretched and grabbed her overnight bag from the front seat. He reached for her hand and tugged her closer. Every shred of Sophie's seasoned resistance melted when he leaned forward. Knowing exactly what he intended to do, she pulled back.

'Sorry,' Charlie apologised, frowning with disappointment. 'Too soon?'

He was handsome, with a winning and gently persuasive nature. What woman could resist? She didn't dare analyse why, because she was drawn by his charisma, too.

'Not at all,' she reassured him hesitantly. 'Just removing these.' She slipped off his glasses, folded them carefully and tucked them into his top shirt pocket. 'As you were.' She couldn't stop herself voicing the enticement or believe she would ever be so forward.

He grinned and tried again. His arms slid with slow and sure possession around her waist and his kiss blew her away. Good thing he held her tight. It wasn't just the taste and feel of his soft mouth eagerly crushing hers, but the deep response that stirred into life right through her whole body. His skin was warm, his hair thick and slightly coarse. Very masculine. To her surprise, all new sensations she adored. He smelt of an enticing spicy aftershave and looked dreamily casual in jeans, a white open-necked shirt, and tweed coat with leather elbow patches.

'Shouldn't we be moving along?' she breathed.

'Sorry. Around you I tend to lose concentration.'

Sophie smiled, smitten by this romantic scientific man. Were they moving too fast? Had she been unfeminine and brazen throwing herself at him? He didn't seem to mind. He caught her hand and led her across to his vehicle, took the bag from her and tossed it into the back.

'It's a long drive. You must be exhausted.'

'I'd appreciate some lunch.'

'Follow me.'

They wandered across to the botanic

gardens nearby but decided against eating in the restaurant. Instead, they grabbed a sandwich and a cool drink and sat on the grass under a tree.

'So, this is home for you,' she said idly, trying to remain unaffected by him and failing.

'My working home, yes.' The breeze blew a lock of hair onto his forehead and the play of light and shade from the overhead leaves reflected in his glasses. Holding back, Sophie discovered, wasn't working. Hard to remain detached. Men had shown interest in her over the years, but she had erected safe defences and discouraged them all, deliberately ending any friendship that strayed beyond casual.

Changing focus, she asked, 'What's the plan for meeting your family?'

'An informal chat with Mother and Amanda. After that, we wing it until dinner.'

'I've brought a huge folder of pictures and notes.'

'Good. Amanda's husband Warren

and their children will be there later. And Father, of course.'

'I didn't book anything. You said you'd arrange accommodation for tonight?' Sophie prompted.

'There's a small boutique hotel in the hills. I thought you'd appreciate that rather than a big impersonal one in the city.'

She marvelled at his thoughtfulness. 'Sounds lovely.'

Sophie sipped her cool drink and watched people walking past to avoid ogling the appealing man seated so close their arms brushed. Somehow she survived and, within half an hour, they were speeding along the freeway into the Adelaide hills. When they drew up before an imposing double-storey lime-stone house behind locked and ornate black iron gates, Sophie drew in a deep breath.

'This is very grand.'

'They don't bite.' Charlie seemed annoyed as he wound down his window, pressed some buttons on a security panel, and the gates slowly slid open.

'I didn't mean — '

'This lifestyle isn't for me either,' he admitted quietly as he pulled up on the circular drive. 'We're civil and keep in touch.' He paused. 'But I'm not close to my family.'

'Why not?'

'They don't approve of my career or understand why a grown man wants to scramble around among rocks for a living.'

Sophie scoffed. 'Your father undoubtedly wears a wig in court, and they think *you're* odd.'

Charlie threw back his head and laughed, which effectively broke the tension.

Behind the bold front, Sophie sensed vulnerability. Yet he had thrust his own personal feelings aside to help her. 'I'm sorry if my coming here has made it hard for you.'

'No problem. I offered. They can help.'

He jumped out and opened her door, leading her toward the house on neatly paved pathways. In the cool of the hills, rhododendrons, azaleas and all manner of lush and leafy bushes flourished. No native plants or gum trees here, Sophie noticed as they walked up the broad steps to the double doors at the entrance. She expected them to go straight in, but Charlie rapped the brass door knocker.

His formality surprised her. On her family's property, Sunday Plains over in the west, doors were never locked. Family, neighbours and friends wandered in and announced themselves. But their approaching dust would have been seen for miles. Far less ceremony in the outback. Sophie regarded Charlie with a side glance. His jaw clenched as a maid opened the door.

'Mister Charles.'

'Sylvia.'

As they were led down a hushed carpeted hall with lofty ceilings, Sophie whispered in concern, clutching her

128

folder, 'I'm only in jeans.'

With a firm hand at her elbow Charlie pulled her to a stop. 'I like you just the way you are,' he murmured.

In that private moment, a sense of calm descended over her and on instinct she kissed him back. On the lips. Which was when his mother caught them.

'Charles, dear.' There was censure and surprise in the crisp tone. She was thin and neatly dressed.

'Mother.' They air-kissed. 'This is Sophie Nash. My mother Anne.'

The sharp hazel eyes regarded her intently. 'Sophie. Welcome to Westerfield.'

'Thank you. This is a magnificent home,' Sophie blurted out, overawed.

Clearly the right thing to say, because Anne Kendall preened. 'We do need space to entertain. Come into the drawing room for tea. Amanda's waiting.'

It proved to be a sumptuous room of deep white sofas and bay windows overlooking a side garden, with a young woman standing before an unlit marble fireplace, her hands clasped behind her back. She was slim like her mother but more casually dressed, Sophie was relieved to see, in black slacks, a silky over-shirt and bare feet. Well, who needed shoes on this thick carpet? Sophie was tempted to discard her own. She relaxed, somehow sensing an ally in Charlie's sister.

At the sight of them, Amanda's face lit up. 'Charlie.' She hurled herself across the room. Brother and sister hugged warmly and he introduced them.

'Charlie tells me you manage a sheep station. Amazing.' Amanda's eyes sparkled with enthusiasm. 'Working on a rustic country project with you — if you decide to go ahead,' she quickly clarified, 'will be a refreshing change from the stainless steel and glass most of my clients demand these days. I try and talk them out of it, but will they listen?'

130

Anne Kendall sat sedately on a sofa and poured tea. A silver tower of delicate cakes, slices, scones and sandwiches graced a carved low table. Alongside was a tray set out with floral English china. Sophie had never taken high tea before.

Amanda patted the seat beside her on the other double sofa, but Charlie remained standing. Without ceremony he grabbed a triangle sandwich and ate it in one mouthful.

'Is the boss about?' he asked.

'In his study. But he won't want to be disturbed,' his mother warned.

'Then I'll go and play with the dog.'

'Don't you want tea?' Anne asked.

'I'd rather have a beer. Trust it's in the billiard room bar fridge as usual. I'll leave you women to it.' He winked at Sophie as he left.

'Is that full of your ideas?' Amanda nodded toward Sophie's folder.

She handed it over and Charlie's sister flipped through. Anne, it seemed, preferred to sit back and observe. Or was that inspect? Sophie wondered.

'Eat,' Amanda urged. 'Dinner's not till eight.'

Sophie balanced her teacup and chose first a sandwich then a dainty cake.

'I can see your vision.' Amanda studied Sophie's concept pages. 'And it seems perfect for what you want to achieve, judging by what Charlie told me. I'll want to see your property, of course, before I source anything.'

'Really?' Sophie nearly squeaked.

'Absolutely. To get a feel for the location and ambience before I commit to any purchases. But I won't buy a thing without your approval. You'd come out too, wouldn't you?' Amanda glanced across at her mother.

Anne Kendall blinked and hesitated. 'I'll check my appointment book,' she said evasively.

'Makes sense to see what you're recommending to your friends,' Amanda said easily. 'Personally I can't wait. And it best be soon. Summer's heating up and Christmas is just around the corner.'

'Precisely,' Anne chimed in self-importantly. 'I believe I have a function or commitment almost every day.'

'Up to you.' Her daughter shrugged. 'But I imagine Sophie's keen to finalise details.' Amanda glanced in her direction. 'I can't move forward until I see what I'm working with.'

'Then perhaps we can discuss it,' Anne conceded, 'and let Sophie know.'

'Great. I'm going to pore over this in the library and make notes.' Amanda rose and tapped Sophie's folder. 'So I'll leave you two to discuss Mother's possibilities.'

Sophie liked Amanda's forthright manner. You knew exactly where you stood with her and she was undoubtedly a formidable businesswoman. Of Anne, she wasn't so sure. But in the end their conversation proceeded smoothly enough. Sophie remembered Charlie's lovely comment earlier in the hallway that he liked her just as she was, and she was determined to be herself.

Anne outlined the groups she was involved with and those most likely to enjoy an artistic week or weekend away. 'If any of them decide to go ahead,' Sophie said, producing a business card from her shoulder bag, 'their representative can contact me by phone or email to make an enquiry or booking.' She explained the comfortable homestead accommodation and the more basic camping option. 'By next autumn and winter tourist season we hope to have renovated our self-catering and B&B cottages.'

'Sounds like you have everything underway.' Anne smiled stiffly.

'Charlie's been a huge help.' She bit her tongue almost as soon as she said it.

After a telling pause and narrowed gaze, his mother asked, 'How exactly did you meet?'

He hadn't told them? Since by his own admission they weren't close, Sophie realised she shouldn't be surprised. 'He led a university geology field camp out on the property in spring. They were washed out and left early. Then when I told Charlie my partner was leaving — '

'You're *involved*?' Anne made it sound distasteful.

Sophie realised she misunderstood the term 'partner', so commonly used in quite another sense these days. 'My partner in the property, Jack Bryce,' she corrected. 'He's returning to the Territory. He disapproved of tourism, actually, and I respected his decision, which is why I haven't developed it sooner. But I strongly believe it's the way forward to keep Casuarina Downs viable into the future.'

'Couldn't agree more.' Charlie ambled into the room, nursing a half-empty glass of beer and grabbing a chocolate slice from the cake tower. Anne caught Sophie beaming at her son's reappearance. 'Where's Amanda?' he asked.

'Library. Why?'

'Warren and the kids are here. They want a swim.'

Thereafter the Kendall mansion exploded into life, and Sophie was puzzled when Anne didn't brighten at the children's arrival. Her own mother erupted into raptures when she saw hers. In her experience, grandparents usually worshipped and spoilt the next generation.

A tiny female voice called out, 'Mummy?' and a small pink whirlwind bolted along the hall.

'In here, darling,' they heard Amanda respond. Then in her booming voice she added, 'Boys! Stop!' She emerged in the library doorway that led off to the left of the front entrance. 'What happened to Grandmother's rule of no running indoors?' The commotion of the arrivals drew everyone into the hall. Anne cleared her throat. 'Children?'

'Grandmother,' they responded politely.

Sophie noticed there were no hugs or kisses. Anne's loss, she felt, with a pang of sorrow on their behalf.

'This is Miss Nash,' Amanda introduced her, by now having scooped up her daughter into her arms.

'How do you do,' the boys chorused.

'Please, call me Sophie,' she said with a smile. The older boy reminded her of her own nephew, her sister Sally's son, Oliver.

'Warren, this is Sophie Nash, Charlie's friend.' She accepted his firm handshake. 'If you children all have your swimmers on under those clothes,' Amanda said as she handed her daughter over to Warren, 'Daddy will take you all out to the pool while we ladies find ourselves a lovely long drink.'

'Of course,' Charlie said. 'Wine okay?'

Amanda and Sophie nodded but Anne said, 'Champagne for me — and for heaven's sake, Charles, go and dig your father out of that study.'

Charlie dutifully disappeared while Warren followed the scampering children outside. Anne trailed after them through French doors at the end of the hall, but Amanda grabbed Sophie's elbow and held her back.

'We were all agog to meet you. Charlie rarely brings home a girlfriend.'

'Oh I'm not sure I can be classed as such. We're just friends,' Sophie protested quickly.

Amanda eyed her curiously. 'Well, anyway, the last one . . . ' She frowned in thought. 'Belle someone. Hyphenated name,' she said absently with a dismissive wave of one hand. 'We only met twice, even though they seemed serious and must have been together almost a year. Gorgeous thing, all legs, but she put on her runners apparently when Charlie mentioned he wanted to live in the bush.' She laughed.

'Oh.' Sophie was concerned to hear it for Charlie's sake.

'You're much more his type.' She lowered her voice and leaned closer. 'Now, roll up your jeans and kick off your shoes,' she insisted as they sauntered out onto a broad sheltered patio paved with freestone and over-looking a crystal-clear aquamarine pool.

Sophie sighed and did as she was told. A moment later Charlie pressed a cold, dewy glass into her hand. Stretched out on a reclining daybed beneath a weeping shady tree with droplets of sunshine peeping through its leaves, and sipping chilled wine, she began to relax, her mood possibly influenced by the fact that Charlie was sprawled out on a lounger beside her. Amanda sat on the other.

Anne sat apart, shaded by an enormously elegant sunhat. Charlie's father still had not yet made an appearance. Warren and the children all squealed and splashed in the heated water: two rowdy schoolboys, Jacob and Daniel, and a cute little preschooler, Charlotte, with a floaty ring around her waist, kicking and laughing as much as her brothers.

Sophie tasted the crisp chilled wine and contemplated the scene. Children.

She'd never considered them for herself. All part of her philosophy over the years of moving between outback station properties, jobs and employers in the guise of gaining experience and saving for a place of her own one day. Which she had achieved. Now what?

Established on Casuarina Downs, she hadn't thought any further ahead until Charlie Kendall unexpectedly entered her life. Sophie had been alarmed to feel restless ever since, and pleasantly shaken at the sight of him, his voice, and now his kisses. He'd openly admitted his attraction and shown his emotions.

And that was where her dilemma lay. Because she had willingly responded. Against all her former practised habits. Now her quandary became, *how to proceed from here?*

'You're very quiet.'

Sophie had closed her eyes in reflection and opened them to respond to Charlie. 'I'm very relaxed actually.' Mostly true. 'I don't usually wind down this much on the station. We tend to potter about doing something seven days a week. And it *was* a long drive this morning.'

'Then I best get you to bed early tonight,' he drawled, a teasing amusement in his voice.

Charlie's meaningful hint, although backed with humour, made Sophie flush with imagination and she was too stumped to reply. She gulped the last of her wine. Then Warren and the children emerged from the pool, dripping and shivering. Amanda wrapped them in towels and muttered something about running bath water. Anne sauntered by and Charlie pushed himself off the lounger.

'I've had your bag taken upstairs to a guest room. We meet in the drawing room by seven for dinner at eight.'

Sophie checked her watch. That gave her almost an hour to collect her thoughts and change.

Charlie sought her hand and led her upstairs. 'Is everything all right?'

'I'm sure it will be.' For the moment anyway, she decided not to fight her emotions. It was too exhausting. Life and fate would take their course as they always did.

'I'll knock on your door around seven.'

She nodded and they parted.

The guest suite was large and comfortable. After a long refreshing shower and a light touch of makeup, Sophie felt like a new person. The peace and break from the family allowed her to gather her composure. And boy was she ever glad at the last minute while packing that she had thought to roll up her pink-and-black-print maxi-dress and jam it into a corner. Thank heavens it hadn't creased. She'd also crammed in a pair of black strappy heels which she seldom wore.

When she opened the door to Charlie's knock, he leaned against the door frame, arms folded, and whistled softly. 'I haven't seen you in a dress before. You look gorgeous.'

She teetered self-consciously on her heels. 'Thank you. Hope I'm dressy enough.'

'You're perfect.' His warm gaze held hers and he took her hand, twining their fingers as they descended the stairs together.

In the drawing room again, Sophie finally met Charlie's distinguished father. He was a greying older version of his son and regarded her with steely observation. He strode toward them, hand outstretched in greeting. 'Son. Sorry I was busy earlier,' he mumbled automatically.

'Father, this is Sophie Nash.'

'Michael,' he insisted. 'Lovely to meet you, my dear.' His voice was cultured but not quite as plummy as his wife's.

Jacob and Daniel wore checked shirts and jeans, while Charlotte was adorable in frothy pink and white. They all sat obediently on a sofa, sipping soft drinks. The adults stood around chatting, Amanda in a short fitted blue cocktail dress with a bright modern necklace, Anne in basic black with pearls, the men all in dress shirts and slacks. Sophie was relieved that her dress code fitted in.

Eventually a maid announced dinner and everyone filed into the grand dining room across the hall, glittering beneath chandeliers and candles, and gleaming with tableware. Michael and Anne took up their seats at either end.

By contrast to the present formality, Sophie noted, growing up on open kilometres of vast outback country, riding horses and motorbikes, Nash family meals and gatherings either took the form of a barbeque or were conducted with far less ceremony around the huge Sunday Plains dining table.

During dinner, Sophie learnt that their home was named for Anne's family home in Berkshire, England: Westerfield Hall, apparently set in hundreds of acres of countryside. That must be the 'pile' Charlie had once mentioned.

'It does have a rather stunning formal courtyard garden out the back if I remember correctly,' Charlie said. Turning to Sophie, he explained, 'Only visited once as a child with the family.'

'My brother, Robert, lives on the estate now,' Anne said proudly. 'Handy to London for business.'

Completely oblivious to the conversation, Charlie's thoughts had strayed to his vocation. 'Berkshire's an interesting region.'

'Plenty of rocks for you to explore, you mean,' Sophie scoffed affectionately.

Their shared glance of warmth and rapport did not pass unnoticed among the family, who exchanged glances.

'Chalk downlands mostly,' he murmured beside Sophie as if speaking to her alone, though she noticed that everyone else politely listened too. 'In the west where Mother's family come from, it's quite rural. Agriculture and

145

racehorse training, the lovely wooded Kennet Valley.'

'Much of it is designated an area of outstanding natural beauty,' Anne intervened importantly, pausing as she ate to take a delicate sip of wine.

'In the ice age,' Charlie went on as if his mother hadn't spoken, 'course we're talking tens of thousands of years ago,' he clarified, 'the Thames and its tributaries deposited sediment of sand and gravel. Today these are quarried for aggregate, and the workings have revealed ancient implements like flint hand axes.'

Sophie grew quite charmed by Charlie's preoccupied moments where he dropped naturally into professional reflection. He was a marvellous repository of knowledge. She began to feel Arcadian and deficient by comparison — all the more pronounced in this lavish setting among the members of this highly educated family. The social gap between herself and Charlie had been totally absent out on

146

Casuarina Downs.

'The local sarsen stones have been used as building material for thousands of years, including Stonehenge. They're found all over Berkshire as gateposts, stepping stones and the like. They were extensively used to build Windsor Castle.'

Besides Sophie, Charlie had at least one other fascinated listener. Jacob had stopped eating and stared at his uncle, completely absorbed, with his chin in his hand. But while everyone politely allowed Charlie to ramble, his parents' eyes had glazed over.

Amanda groaned. 'Charlie, must we? Jacob, elbows off the table, darling,' she corrected him. Her son quickly obeyed and shovelled in the rest of the food on his plate.

The break in Charlie's discourse allowed conversation to move on to other subjects. After a salad starter, Sophie's measured portion of tender fillet steak and artistically prepared side of steamed vegetables was only upstaged by a rich chocolate mousse served in elegant crystal dishes.

The children were bundled off to bed soon after dinner while the adults took coffee in the drawing room. Somewhere before eleven, Charlie caught Sophie stifling a yawn. Aware of her early start that morning, he tactfully rose to excuse them. Sophie dashed upstairs to retrieve her bag from the guest room. When she descended to the entry hall, Charlie was nowhere to be seen, but she heard murmured voices further along. Strolling closer to investigate, she discovered it was from the library, its huge panelled door ajar.

Recognising Charlie's voice, Sophie moved forward to let him know she was ready but stopped on the threshold, turning cold at the mention of her name in his mother's crisp tone.

'I take it Miss Nash is more than a friend, Charles.' Anne was probing and did not sound pleased.

'You've never cared about my friends in the past, Mother. Why start now?' he said bluntly, and Sophie gasped at his sharp challenge. 'But, yes,' he continued, 'Sophie is a very special woman and I'm hoping she becomes much more than a friend.'

He was? Sophie blushed.

'What about Belle?' Anne asked. The girlfriend in his recent past. Sophie sensed his hesitation to reply.

'What about her?'

'She was much more than a friend, too, surely?'

'Not soon enough. We let our passion come before friendship,' he said honestly. 'I won't make that same mistake again.'

Sophie endured a flash of unreasonable jealousy to think of Charlie and this Belle woman together.

'But Miss Nash is just a *farmer*, Charles,' Anne complained. Sophie stifled an offended gasp.

'So were my grandparents,' she heard Charlie respond crisply.

Anne scoffed. 'It was only a hobby farm when they retired. He'd had a professional career all his life.'

'Uncle Robert's a *farmer*, as you put it, back in England,' Charlie disputed with a sharp chuckle of wry humour at his mother's expense.

'He employs workers,' she argued. 'He's a businessman.'

'Only because his little *farm* of, what, forty acres won't support him and that crumbling pile he lives in.'

'Westerfield Hall is my family home.' Anne clearly took exception to his criticism.

'Well,' Charlie drawled, 'Sophie's *farm*,' he expressed carefully, 'is actually a pastoral sheep station of some five hundred square kilometres.'

Sophie smiled to herself. She hoped that small fact lifted Anne's carefully plucked eyebrows. She wanted to cheer Charlie's support.

The stunning truth clearly made no impact because his mother quickly appealed, 'You should see Belle again.'

'What for?'

'Maybe you'll feel differently now.

You two made a stunning couple.'

'Thanks, but no thanks,' came his swift reply.

Sophie heard movement from the library. Afraid of being caught eavesdropping, she stumbled backward.

'Everything all right?' Sophie jumped when Michael approached quietly behind her. 'Sorry, didn't mean to startle you.'

Clutching her bag with a knuckle-white grip, she managed to pull a smile. 'I'm just tired. Waiting for Charlie to say good night to his mother.' And listen to herself being verbally torn to shreds. Utterly demoralising. She wished Charlie would appear. She just wanted to leave.

As if reading her thoughts, Michael stepped across the hall and pushed the library door fully open. Charles and his mother turned at his entrance to see Sophie standing behind him. She caught Charlie's gaze and was surprised to see his face set grimly with anger.

She had never seen him irate before. In that instant, he knew she had overheard their conversation. She longed to rush over and hug him for defending her against his own flesh and blood. To tell him it didn't matter. That she understood.

Totally detached from anything she had just said, and making a remarkable turnabout, Anne briskly approached, suddenly all smiles and civility. 'Sophie, it's been lovely to meet you.'

She bristled at the woman's duplicity. *Yet you hope you never have to see me again.* Shaking with indignation, Sophie chose her words carefully. 'I appreciate your hospitality,' was all she could manage. 'Michael, a pleasure to meet you,' she pointedly complimented him. No doubt he buried himself in his study to avoid his wife, she thought unkindly.

'Any time, my dear,' he said quietly, shades of Charlie's gentlemanly strength mirrored in his voice and manner.

'Good night, Father.' The men shook

hands, but Charles only tossed indifferently over his shoulder, 'Mother.'

As useful and eventful as the day had been, it had also been a long one, especially for Sophie. She released a long sigh of relief as they drove away from the Kendall mansion. She and Charlie were silent in the car as they wound through the hills to their overnight accommodation. She thought he wasn't going to raise the sticky library scene until they pulled up before a beautiful old freestone house that was now a boutique hotel.

He parked, turned off the engine and sighed, rubbing a weary hand across his face. 'I won't apologise for my mother. Everyone knows she's a snob.'

Sophie noted the anguish and disappointment in his voice. 'Fortunately her son isn't,' she said kindly. 'Thank you for being my knight.'

'I only spoke the truth. Sadly, my mother didn't. A legacy of an indulged upbringing and grander times that no longer exist. She's clinging to memories.'

'Every family has cracks in their façade, no matter how exalted they might claim to be.'

He scowled. 'Mother has more than most. I do appreciate your tolerance. Your attitude is more than generous.'

Sophie glowed at his words but would never divulge to him the cringing depth of hurt she still felt from Anne's cutting words and the insinuation that she was unacceptable in their social circle. Disapproval noted. She puzzled over why she should be so deeply bothered by Anne's lack of acceptance. After all, she and Charlie were only friends, and she was only here because he had offered her a business favour. In hindsight perhaps she should have refused, but then she would never have met Michael and Amanda, both charming inclusive people who justified the visit and made it worthwhile.

Charles carried their bags up the short flight of steps to reception. He had arranged an indulgent, comfortable suite for her, but when he lingered just inside her door for a prolonged and stirring good-night kiss he gave the impression of great reluctance to leave.

Deeply affected by its impact, Sophie was barely aware of her surroundings after he had gone. She merely slid out of her clothes and fell into bed.

* * *

She awoke to beams of sunlight across her room and realised in her combined euphoria and exhaustion last night she had forgotten to draw the curtains. After a quick shower, and because the weather was so warm now in late spring, she abandoned jeans and opted for denim Capris and a tailored pink shirt, slipping her feet into loafers.

When she flung open her French doors onto a tiled balcony terrace running the length of the lovely old double-storey building, it was to discover stunning views of the hills and valleys beyond. And Charlie reading the *Sunday Mail* at a table laid out with breakfast. He looked dynamic and appealing in beige cargos and a black T-shirt with the collar turned up. Very urban, she thought, admiring him for longer than she would normally dare.

He glanced up and smiled. 'Morning. Good sleep?'

'Wonderful.' She approached and hungrily eyed the juices, fruits and toast. 'Do we share?'

'Absolutely,' he drawled, and gestured for her to join him.

Sophie noted he had already eaten, and the aroma of strong black coffee drifted to her from his half-empty cup. She sat opposite, draped a linen napkin over her knees, and lifted the lids on the domed silver dishes.

'Scrambled eggs, lashings of bacon, and baked tomatoes. After our feast last night, I shouldn't have an appetite.'

He flashed her a devilish grin. 'Refreshing to see a woman enjoy her food and not just push lettuce leaves around her plate.'

Sophie always enjoyed food and, living an active outdoor life, had never really needed to watch her weight. 'This is a gorgeous old place. So much charm and character,' she said, pouring juice while she decided what to eat first.

'It was originally built by a wealthy early settler as a summer residence. Much cooler up here in the hills than down in the city.'

Conversation became guarded again, with Sophie feeling the pressure and excitement of their intimate situation. She wanted to let herself go and experience every wonderful moment of tenderness swelling up inside when she and Charlie were together, but a suspicious faceless little spirit was sitting on her shoulder, shielding her heart and warning her that men disappeared from your life and she should retreat. Plus there was the added caution after his mother's aspersions last night.

An hour later, they checked out. With

no idea of their destination, Sophie was not surprised when they headed west and soon reached the beach. Charlie lived around here somewhere. They passed a surf club and a café in an area of comfortable homes and stunning apartment blocks facing the sea to their right, with cycle paths and low sand dunes on their left. They slowed and turned into the driveway of a neat modern two-storey building.

'Fabulous view,' Sophie breathed, sweeping her gaze over the ocean as she alighted from the vehicle. 'Quite a contrast to where I live.'

'Do you have time for the grand tour and a walk on the beach?'

She wrinkled her nose and said playfully, 'I have a few hours. Let's be devils and cram it all in.' His adoring smile in response made her heart tumble.

Charlie's apartment was modern, with walls of glass across the front entry lobby giving an uninterrupted view of sparkling blue waters. He caught her hand and led her along a short, narrow passage and up a flight of stairs. The place was not so much untidy as occupied.

'My housekeeper comes in once a week,' he said apologetically.

Quick as a flash and with an impish grin, Sophie quipped, 'Don't worry, I like you just the way you are.'

Charlie chuckled. Their gazes drifted together and held in accord before he led her through the rest of his home.

From the upper living area Sophie glimpsed even better views out to sea. Well-thumbed copies of *National Geographic* and *TAG* magazines were stacked on a sideboard with photos of rocky landscapes on the covers. They were obviously associated with his profession. Glancing aside, she spied a fat glass jar filled with smooth round pebbles, bits of coloured rocks and sea shells, and remembered Charlie's mention of a childhood collection his grandfather had saved. She ran her hand over it as she passed. 'Your finds,' she murmured. 'That must bring back memories.'

'Every day.' He eyed them fondly. From the time he had spoken of them, Sophie guessed his grandparents had left a lasting impression on his life.

'Well.' She turned away and looked out across the street to his stunning sea view. 'This might not be the bush or the outback, but the ocean's a kind of frontier. You're about as far as you can get across the city from your parents,' she teased.

He shrugged easily. 'Wasn't a conscious choice. Just looking for a space on earth where I could feel comfortable and make my own life,' he admitted quietly. She sensed him moving up quietly behind her. 'I'm beginning to discover I probably have all I need right here,' he said softly.

She was deeply moved by his confession but battled to keep her feelings under control. Filled with confusion when his arms stole around her, she lost the struggle and turned in to him, needing and expecting to be kissed.

'That's more like it,' Charlie declared afterwards with a contented sigh. 'Let's blow away the cobwebs. Want to feel the sand between your toes?'

They returned downstairs and ran across the street to the foreshore footpath. 'I often cycle along here,' Charlie told her. 'Up to Henley Beach and Largs Bay, or down to Glenelg or Brighton.'

'Do you wear those lycra bike shorts?' she taunted, grinning.

'Afraid so,' he admitted, looking sheepish. Then he turned thoughtful. 'Bikes are extraordinarily efficient, you know.'

'Really.' Sophie pretended riveting interest and tried not to laugh. She just knew that look and that he was about to share another nugget of trivia.

'Bicycles are the most efficient self-powered means of transportation,' he declared. 'Ninety-nine percent of energy into the pedals goes to the wheels.'

'Amazing,' she said wryly. 'How fast can *you* go?' she challenged.

Charlie shrugged. 'With a good run, maybe up to thirty kilometres an hour.'

Sophie scoffed. 'With a tail wind.'

'Racing bikes are even faster.'

Knowing they could outstrip a cyclist any day, Sophie said, 'I'll bet an emu could give you a run for your money.'

He laughed. 'Okay, you win. I'm whipped.'

They descended the wooden steps over the dunes and down onto the broad stretch of white sand. The midday sun shimmered a path across the water and the lacy white froth of small waves rolled continually ashore.

Sophie stood shielding her gaze with a hand over her eyes out to the Gulf, her long hair flying out behind her in the stiff salt-laden breeze. She inhaled deeply to savour it. She would be back home in the outback soon enough. 'You have all this water on your doorstep,' she marvelled.

'Bit different to Casuarina, for sure.

I'll bet we both see some awesome sunsets.'

They walked for a while, not talking, drawn to the water's edge to remove their shoes and paddle in the shallows, Sophie all too aware that her time in the city was running out. 'Thanks for organising this weekend,' she said eventually. 'Your family. The hotel last night. I don't think I've ever felt so completely taken care of and spoiled.'

'Perhaps no one has ever cared enough,' he suggested quietly.

A moment of electric magnetism passed between them like a current.

'Maybe,' Sophie whispered, so unnerved by Charlie's tender gaze she almost forgot to breathe and looked away, desperate to break the connection.

'Do you feel something kicking into play between us?'

By now their pace had slowed and they sauntered shoulder to shoulder, the languid waves washing over their bare feet. Charlie stopped in the shallows and pulled her against him.

'Sophie?' he prompted.

'You're a dangerous man.'

'No more than you with a rifle beside you in the ute.'

She laughed. 'I have a licence for it and it's on private property. I was thinking of a rather more different kind of dangerous.'

'To your feelings?' he murmured as he wound his arms around her waist. Tight.

'You're very attentive, Charlie, and appealing. I'm finding it difficult to leave.'

'Then don't.'

His low voice and blatant dare blitzed any other challenge Sophie had ever faced in her life. And she knew he meant it. He wanted her. But she had never really been in any doubt. He had made his interest clear right from the beginning, with meaningful glances sent her way at their first meeting.

'I had no idea scientists could be so romantic.'

'Feeling threatened?'

She swallowed. 'Something like that.'

'Is that a good thing?'

'It's certainly new for me.'

'Because you're hiding yourself away in the outback so no one can find you?'

Sophie dipped her head self-consciously. His remark cut awfully close to the truth. Was she so transparent? She held back her surprise that an intellectual could be so tapped into feelings. She looked away over his shoulder but he tipped one finger gently beneath her chin, tilting her face back to him. Then he bent and slowly, deliberately, kissed her again.

Sophie only felt and cared about the warm touch of his mouth against hers, her passion deepening, the rush of waves lapping over their feet and around their ankles. Her arms snaked up around his neck and his big firm hands spread over her back, holding her tight as the real world fell away and they entered their own.

'What happens now?' Charlie asked

after a while, waiting for Sophie to respond.

Her chest tightened. 'What are we talking about here?'

'Whatever you want it to be. Consider me already on board,' he said openly.

'You're not making this easy.' She drew away, looked down and scuffed her toes into the sand. 'What do *you* want exactly?' As if she didn't know. But she stalled for time.

'You. To take our relationship further and see where it leads,' he admitted easily.

Sophie's gaze snapped up to his shadowed face backlit by the sun, and her whole body froze with fear. 'My word, Dr. Kendall, no pressure.'

'You're surprised?' He frowned in confusion.

'You recently broke up with Belle,' she pointed out, scrambling for any reason to justify her reluctance. She felt mean for suggesting, 'This isn't a rebound?'

He looked offended and ground his jaw. 'That relationship is well over,' he said firmly.

For the first time ever, Sophie felt trapped. Completely betrayed by her body and heart, she reverted to her usual defence strategy and began building a wall. It had always worked in the past. How had her friendship with Charlie progressed this far without being checked like she was normally able to do? She knew, of course. Because her will to resist Charlie was different than with all the others. There was a chemistry. He was warm and smart and thoughtful, but right now she didn't have a satisfactory answer for him. Their romance was hurtling along at a great speed and Sophie felt neither prepared nor ready for it.

As though standing on hot sand, she stepped away from him. 'I'll need to think about it,' she mumbled.

He shook his head. 'You don't feel the same?' Anxiety and disbelief filtered into his voice.

Terrified of a confrontation and any pressure to commit, Sophie stilled, her throat dry. Love meant heartbreak, losing those you cared about, and she wasn't going there. She had seen it first-hand and it had devastated the people involved. Impossible to explain that to Charlie without looking foolish. Because it meant she lacked courage, and she'd never thought of herself as a coward.

Seeing the depth of disappointment in his eyes, Sophie stammered, 'I'm just saying . . . I need more time.'

'Don't take too long,' he said gruffly. After a tense, awkward moment he said, 'I'll drive you back to the university to get your ute.'

'Of course. Thank you.'

Sophie trailed behind, feeling like a wayward child. Her indecision had hurt him when her kisses clearly relayed a different message. He had a right to be confused. Had she been unfair to encourage him? But her feelings had developed so quickly and beyond all her expectations. And now he was asking for some kind of promise between them which, through dread, she was reluctant to give.

It remained unspoken but it was clear they were both falling in love here — one of them grudgingly. The sensation was like an unstoppable roller coaster. Nothing you could do about it but enjoy the ride and wait for the destination. And that was a most terrifying reality. How could Sophie commit to anything or pledge her love when she just knew disaster loomed ahead?

'Speak of the devil,' Charlie muttered as they crested the top of the dunes and glanced toward his apartment.

Sophie wanted to melt into the pavement. Draped over the bonnet of a sleek white convertible with its soft black top down was the most gobsmackingly gorgeous Hollywood siren she had ever seen. Seemed Dr. Charlie Kendall had a thing for blondes.

Any wonder Charlie's mother considered the glamorous woman more socially suitable for her son? Sophie felt like a mouse in comparison and shrivelled from inside, but at least her own hair colour was natural and didn't come out of a bottle. This could only be Belle.

The visitor narrowed her daggered gaze at Sophie as they approached. 'Charles, darling. You kept me waiting.' She leaned forward and kissed him full and possessively on the mouth in a waft of strong perfume.

He seemed irritated. 'I wasn't expecting you.'

The woman glared at Sophie. 'Clearly.'

Teetering on heels and still clinging to Charlie, she looked down at his companion with disdain, deciding after a long, critical stare that she was no competition. 'And who do we have here?'

Charlie heaved an impatient sigh of resignation, seeming unimpressed. But

Sophie couldn't determine with whom. 'Mirabelle Spencer-Holmes, Sophie Nash.'

'Charmed.' Belle pulled a tight smile then immediately turned her attention back to Charlie. 'Charles darling, if you have a moment, we need to talk.' She pressed herself close against him and half-turned her shoulder, cleverly excluding Sophie. Charlie leaned sideways and darted an anxious glance at Sophie, the sun glinting off his glasses. He seemed about to say something.

Seizing a chance to escape, Sophie withdrew her mobile phone from the pocket of her Capris and pressed numbers, flashing a false bright smile. 'I'll call a taxi.'

Frowning, he protested, 'Sophie . . . your ute — '

'No bother. I'll make my own way back into the city. Thank you for everything,' she added, meaning it and holding those lovely dark brown eyes for one last tantalising brief moment.

She stepped further away when

Charlie made a move to stop her. The call answered and she gave her address. She smiled and waved him away. 'You go on. They'll be here in five minutes.'

In the face of her determination, Charlie relented, but she could see he was imprisoned and torn. Even as she felt heartened by his conflict, Belle still gripped him with a fierce and selfish control.

'I'll wait until the taxi arrives,' he offered.

'Please don't,' she begged, sending him an appealing loaded glance, trusting him to interpret the underlying meaning in her plea.

He caught on, bless him, gave a brief nod and turned his attention to Belle. Sophie heard them talking as she sauntered away.

★ ★ ★

Charlie had intended to snub Belle, having no problem with leaving her to cool those dangerous stilettos while he

172

ran Sophie back to the university. But his captivating outback woman seemed only too happy to escape. Fast. He still puzzled over her mixed messages. But he fully intended to resume their conversation where it had floundered. Sophie's kisses told him one thing; her baffling fearful reactions relayed another. He would need to give some thought to the reason why. At their first meeting when he asked about her parents, she had become upset at the mention of her father and his early death. Had to be a connection. He figured she would confide in her own time but, for now, he felt powerless to help.

At the sound of an approaching vehicle, he turned and watched the woman of his heart scramble into a taxi and drive away.

'Charlie?' Belle vied for his attention. 'Care for a spin?' She nodded toward her car.

He didn't plan on spending any longer in her company than necessary.

He shook his head. 'Inside,' he scowled and led the way.

'Mother sent you,' he accused bluntly when they were upstairs. It wasn't a question.

Belle pouted. 'She thought it better to nip your little friendship in the bud.'

'Better for who?' he snapped. The Kendall name no doubt. 'I choose my own friends.' He made a note to schedule in that long-overdue chat with his mother.

'Never hurts to have a second opinion,' she argued.

'I make my own decisions.' He pushed out an exasperated sigh, just about over women for today. First Sophie's odd behaviour, then his mother's interference, and now Belle. How much could a man take in one day?

'She is rather *rustic*,' Belle noted. Unfairly, Charlie considered, on five minutes' acquaintance. She couldn't be further from the truth. He bristled at the stinging criticism.

'Not at all.' He smiled to himself, his reflections filling with images of Sophie that easily sprang to mind. 'She's actually one helluva woman and owns an outback sheep station.'

Unimpressed, Belle wrinkled her nose. 'Really.' Disliking any female competition but knowing her own charisma and power, she changed focus and prowled closer. 'Still wearing those annoying glasses, I see. You haven't taken up my suggestion of contact lenses.'

'I'm fine with them.'

She hesitated, perhaps aware she was losing ground. 'I miss *us*.' She brushed a hand through his hair. 'Sometimes.'

'*You* broke it off, remember. I've moved on, Belle. I suggest you do the same.'

'Oh I have.' She smirked. 'Just doing a favour for your mother.'

Charlie seethed with anger that Sophie felt obliged to leave. For nothing.

'Maybe your little bush girl's right for you after all.'

'For heaven's sake, don't tell Mother.'

Belle gave a throaty chuckle. 'Wouldn't dare. Promise.' She eyed him nostalgically. 'Makes me realise we were *this* close to a mistake.' She snapped her fingers.

Charlie shook his head. Belle had a certain earthiness and he had been easily attracted, but it turned out they didn't want the same things and began to disagree, which opened up cracks in their relationship. Over time, the cracks became canyons that neither of them bothered to bridge. Including his long-held dream to live in the country.

'We made a striking couple,' he admitted. 'And I almost proposed.'

She pressed a manicured hand against his T-shirt. 'And I'm glad you didn't.' Her voice lowered seductively. 'Because I would have had to refuse. Lovely seeing you again, Charles.' She pressed a warm kiss on his cheek and threw him a cheeky grin over her shoulder as she left. 'I know my way out.'

★   ★   ★

For Sophie, the trip home was a nightmare. Left alone with her thoughts for four hours, she resorted to singing loudly along with the radio, pretending to enjoy the scenery but generally feeling a gloom she couldn't shake. Any other woman would have welcomed Charlie's hint like a shot and not hesitated to take their relationship further, especially feeling about him the way she did. But she had conceded to her long-held fears of losing the ones she loved, so that her head and heart fought each other.

Turning off the main road and hitting the gravel to Casuarina Downs for once gave her none of the usual elation she felt when returning home. Arriving back seemed like landing on another planet or arriving in a foreign place, for she had left part of herself back in

Adelaide with Charlie.

Her deep feelings for him were too strong to ignore. She just couldn't admit it yet. Decision time, she knew, one way or the other, was inevitable. Whether to take a leap of faith or ignore her heart. Then again, Belle had made a grand entrance onto the scene. What if Charlie turned to her for comfort and she was back in his life to stay? He hadn't looked thrilled by her unexpected appearance, which Sophie had used to swiftly retreat.

At least Alice was pleased to see her when she walked into the homestead kitchen. And she immediately felt a keen sense of safety and belonging.

'Billie and Jack not coming in for dinner?' she asked later when her housekeeper only served up two plates for the meal.

'Maybe having cookout?' Alice replied vaguely with a shrug.

It was unlike her not to know what went on around the property. She either knew it or sensed it before anyone else.

Sophie thought it odd but let it pass. Later, after catching up with bookwork in the office, she didn't feel ready for sleep yet. Her mind was in too much of a whirl over Charlie's declaration on the beach to concentrate. She could hardly take her romantic troubles to Jack but he had always been a good ear, whether over a tin mug of strong bush tea around a campfire in the past or, these days, a mug of coffee in the cottage.

Sophie strolled toward the light streaming from his open windows across the homestead yard in the dark. Her hand was raised to knock when she heard voices. Jack had company. Since Alice had already gone to bed, there was only one other person it could be. Sophie frowned, instinct making her hesitant to intrude, but their chatty voices carried and she shamelessly lingered to listen.

'Thanks for confiding in me, Jack. Anyone can see Sophie is special to you.' There was a pause. 'I can help you lick your wounds,' Billie coaxed.

Sophie's mouth gaped. Jack had opened up to this slip of a girl? That must have pushed his personal boundaries to its limits. Maybe Billie had prodded. And she was now offering herself! Sophie grinned to herself. The cheeky young thing. Maybe she had been trailing Jack these past months for a very genuine reason other than learning the ropes around the property. She'd certainly seemed besotted by the older man at first glance. Sophie eagerly listened for his reply.

'You're barely out of your teens. I'm over thirty,' he scoffed.

Sophie knew the tone of that feeble objection. It meant nothing. In fact, she would be willing to bet Jack was equally infatuated with Billie, but would fight rather than admit it. He always kept his deepest feelings close — the reason Sophie hadn't twigged his affections for her sooner. But she had seen his occasional quick glance of admiration in Billie's direction more than once since the girl's arrival. At first she'd thought it was just the jillaroo's youth and idolatry of a handsome and experienced outback man; but, based on what she was hearing, it looked like becoming much more.

'I like mature men, not boys,' Billie chuckled. 'Besides, do you think I planned to fall for a geriatric? Love chooses *us*, Tiger, not the other way around.'

How could someone so young be so wise? Sophie marvelled, giving her pause to consider her own feelings and situation with Charlie.

'It would never work,' Jack objected, his voice unconvincing.

'Didn't figure you for a coward, Bryce,' she teased.

This upfront young woman was exactly what Jack needed, Sophie realised. Grounded firmly in her own family and an accomplished outback worker, she would be a good match for him.

'You know I'm not sticking around much longer. I'm moving back to the

Territory.' His objections were weak. When had Billie's *Tiger* become such a kitten?

'I've lived in a caravan and under the stars most of my life. I have no ties,' she reasoned frankly, and Sophie imagined Billie perhaps giving an easy undaunted shrug.

Jack must be interested or he wouldn't be listening. When he heard something he didn't like, he walked away. Sophie was amazed Billie had moved this far with him after knowing him such a short while. But hadn't she herself been intrigued by a certain geologist at first sight?

'You've just signed on here at Casuarina Downs. Sophie's relying on you,' Jack argued loyally.

'She's a strong woman. When she knows the situation, she'll understand.'

There was a break in the conversation. Jack was probably thinking. Sophie shook her head in the half-light, still not believing this unlikely match could happen. She crossed her fingers for them.

'At least let's give it a shot,' Billie said, softer now.

Sophie wondered if they were sitting on the sofa together. Jack murmured something she missed. Billie squealed. Jack said louder, 'Not making any promises, kiddo.'

'Don't expect any,' came her fast reply, her voice high with excitement. 'We should tell Sophie.'

'No hurry. Nothing to tell yet.'

'But I'll be leaving, too. It's only fair it should be soon. Give her plenty of warning.'

Sophie grinned as she crouched beneath the open cottage window. Jack and Billie! Who knew? Compared to her own pathetic situation where she had withdrawn, riddled with doubt, these two unlikely souls had jumped straight in. Even reluctant Jack. Sophie was flattened by a huge sense of personal weakness, making her feel lonelier than ever.

Although amazed by this new turn of

events, she was also delighted for her long-time mate. And relieved, for he could now move on in life with his own family, which she had always believed he needed.

Damn. She suddenly realised the implications. Now she not only needed to find a new business partner in the coming months, but hire another jillaroo or workman as well.

Conversation from inside the cottage stopped. Sophie considered what *might* be happening, but she wasn't about to peer in the window to find out. Time to scamper before she was discovered.

* * *

First thing next day, Sophie arranged a round table discussion for that evening to update everyone on her Adelaide visit. Meanwhile a long day stretched ahead for her, knowing Jack's future was resolved but not her own. With shearing over and summer approaching, her time was less pressured; so to clear her brain, which felt as thick as an outback dust storm, Sophie headed for the kennels.

Drover thumped his tail with delight and darted around her ankles when she released him from his chain, and responded with adoring half-closed eyes when she patted him and ruffled his head and ears. Why couldn't all devotion be this uncomplicated? She ended up running out the track to the main road to clear away the cobwebs, Drover racing happily alongside.

The dilemma of Charlie's suggestion still remained. He was serious about her and she knew it. And, scarily, her feelings for him were returned. She just couldn't free them. This stage was usually when Sophie broke away, ended it and moved on. Although men rarely got this far, because she discouraged them. And it usually worked. This time, in the deepest corner of her heart, she wanted to give in but simply couldn't do it, even knowing what she would lose. She almost feared rejecting Charlie more than flinging herself into his arms, which she so desperately longed to do. So why didn't she?

He would expect a response soon. A dreamy stud like Charlie Kendall wouldn't be on the market for long. If she walked away from him, another hot-blooded woman would snap him up.

Just when she needed a friend, Charlie Kendall had happened along. He was not the man she would have chosen for herself. In actual fact, she wouldn't have gone out and chosen any bloke. She avoided pain by not getting involved in the first place.

She returned to the house pleasantly sapped but no closer to a decision. She showered, then drove out around the property exploring every cottage and partial ruin for renovation potential. Jack found her. His radar had always locked onto hers, so it was no surprise when she noticed his approach in a cloud of dust down the track on the quad bike. He pulled up where Sophie was scrambling among the rubble, determining whether this stony shell of a building was worth saving.

Without a word they sat down in the shade of a half-wall on a wide windowsill, empty now minus its glass and frame but with a stunning view. The early settlers sure knew how to pick a site for a home. Had he chosen this quiet place to tell her about Billie?

For the first time Sophie saw her good friend in a new light. She was bursting to let him know she knew about Billie, although she wasn't proud of the way she found out; but it was right he told her himself in his own time.

He puzzled her by asking bluntly, 'What's up?'

Sophie pulled back warily at his question and frowned. 'Pardon?'

'You're unhappy.'

So no confidences about Billie, then. Instead he had turned the spotlight on her, and it shattered her composure. 'I'm fine,' she insisted. 'Just have a lot on my mind.'

'We all do,' he countered. 'I'm leaving end of summer. My life's changing, too.' He paused, adding quietly, 'But what's the real problem for you? You've been either quiet or crabby lately. My guess is Charlie.'

Sophie sucked in a quick breath. When did this bush man get to be so perceptive? But then they'd become attuned to each other after years of working together.

'Sorry I'm not the best company. I'll try and do better.' She avoided answering his question and addressing the romantic situation in her own life.

'You need to face it and fix it, Soph. We all have tough decisions to make sometimes.' He squinted out across the browning countryside to the red-faced rocky surrounding ranges. He was telling her there comes a time when you have change thrust upon you. Funny that it should be happening for both of them at the same time.

Sophie shrugged. 'Can't do much about it right now.'

'You sure about that?'

She couldn't answer, because she knew she could solve her dilemma by simply picking up the phone.

Having raised the issue and given his firm opinion — how the tables had turned, Sophie thought with a cringe — Jack jumped down from the windowsill and eyeballed the ruin. 'What do you think?'

Sophie rubbed her arms, grateful for the reprieve. 'It has character and it's in a lovely spot. I'm thinking it's worth it.'

He turned a steady gaze on her and said dryly, 'Probably best to go with your instinct then.'

Sophie slid down off the wall and dusted off the seat of her jeans. She knew what he was hinting but ignored his remark because she couldn't face the implications.

'I know you won't be around beyond autumn, but I appreciate your help and staying on even though you don't agree with all this.'

Jack Bryce actually grinned. 'No problem.'

★   ★   ★

That night, Jack and Billie joined them for a late dinner. Feeling down and exhausted, Sophie put on a brave face, smiled, ignored her private upheaval and focused on being positive and bubbly about the future of tourism for the property. She tried to sound upbeat about possibilities and arrangements, and informed them of the Kendall women's imminent visit of appraisal.

At the round-table kitchen conference later, the mood was companionable. Jack and Billie shared warm glances. Somehow the girl had always managed to sit next to him, even on first arrival, and Sophie now knew why. Alice had contacted her tribal elders about conducting the sacred canyon and rock-art tours. Sophie mentioned Charlie's family's offer to help and warned about their imminent visitors.

'Our first priority has to be cleaning the homestead guest rooms until they sparkle. Alice and I can do that. Jack, can you and Billie start sorting out the workshop?'

Billie beamed with pleasure at the thought of working together, no doubt, but Jack stayed silent.

When he didn't object, Sophie said, 'I'll take that as a yes. And I'll keep moving around the property and inspecting the cottages and ruins, make notes and contact a builder in Hawker or Quorn for assessments on the viability of rebuilding them.' She let out a long sigh of responsibility. 'I guess that's all we need for now. If everyone can finish their jobs this week, I'd appreciate it.'

* * *

Within days Sophie took the phone call she was expecting. She had presumed it would be Amanda, but Charlie phoned instead. It would have been far less stressful talking to his sister.

At the sound of his voice, always so warm and comforting, everything unravelled inside her. Damn the man. He completely disturbed her poise. Reason flew out the window and her best intentions dissolved.

'Morning,' she returned his greeting.

It was early. Was he calling from his lovely beachside apartment, or the university? It made him feel closer and seem even more familiar now, having seen where he lived and worked, and being able to picture it in her mind.

'Just following up on that possible weekend for Amanda and Mother to come out. They suggested this weekend or next. Their schedules are booked up after that until Christmas.'

No mention that he would be joining them. Sophie's mood took a hit of deflation. Well, she *had* discouraged him. What else did she expect? And there was always the spectre of Belle in the background.

'The following weekend would suit us better. Give us more time to prepare.'

'Fine. I'll pass it on.'

An awkward interval yawned open when neither of them spoke.

'Sophie,' Charlie said carefully, 'there's a small complication.'

Oh my God, here it comes, she thought. So far Charlie hadn't mentioned the state of their relationship, how they had parted. Was he giving her the shove? Her mouth went dry.

'Dad and Warren are working on a big case at the moment. Amanda would need to bring the children. Is that a problem?'

Sophie sank with relief. That was all. 'Goodness, no,' she said with genuine enthusiasm. 'That would be wonderful. Tell everyone to bring their oldest, toughest gear, a big hat and sensible shoes.'

So except for the menfolk, the entire family was coming, including Anne.

Sophie didn't know whether to be delighted or daunted. She just needed to make a good impression. This was the start of a new direction for Casuarina Downs.

While Sophie would welcome Amanda's ideas, Anne was an unknown quantity. She could only trust she was impressed enough by the landscape to recommend it to her friends. The intense colours over the ridges as the last burst of light struck them at sunset. The softly folding surrounding hills. The peaceful environment of the quiet billabongs and gorges. The informality and oasis of her outback homestead.

Positive reactions to her property were vital. Successful tourism, and cash flow, depended on it.

'Are you still there?' Charlie asked over her deep thoughts.

'Yes. Just hoping it all goes well,' she reassured him quickly.

'I'll confirm it with you in a day or so, then.'

Sophie wondered why Amanda hadn't

made the arrangements. 'Great.'

When she hung up, her hand on the phone was shaking.

* * *

Within twenty-four hours, Charlie phoned back and the date was set. Despite being organised, it still threw Sophie into a renewed flurry of activity. She needed everything to run smoothly and be faultless. This was a test, a trial run for the real thing, and she was determined to get it right. She wanted the Kendall experience to be that of any future paying guests.

The guest rooms, with French doors opening onto the veranda and lace curtains, were meticulously spring cleaned; menus were planned and a rough itinerary for escorting the women around the appropriate areas of the property arranged.

On the Saturday morning of their expected arrival, Sophie paced as the hours slipped by. She double-checked everything. Their arrival time came and passed and she worried they had come to grief.

But then a reassuring phone call came from Amanda. 'Sorry it's taking us so long. We've stopped a few times to let the children out for a scamper, so we're behind schedule. There's only so many times you can replay the same DVD,' she explained, laughing. 'Uncle Charlie is being very patient.'

Charlie was coming! How on earth was she supposed to respond to him when they met again?

Within thirty minutes, a trail of dust along the track into the homestead from the main road signalled their arrival.

In the eruption of multiple human beings emptying themselves from the four-wheel drive, Sophie glimpsed Charlie unloading baggage from the roof rack. Her heart lifted. It was good to see him again, but why had he come? Surely there was no need.

The women greeted each other.

Amanda with her usual spontaneous hug. Anne remained aloof, but that was nothing new. Sophie was just surprised she had condescended to come at all to visit a *farmer*. She reined in her resentment and smiled instead. Good practice for future guests. So far, so good. But then Charlie emerged from behind them and caught her gaze. He moved forward and kissed her on the cheek. 'Sophie,' he murmured.

'I wasn't sure you were coming,' she floundered, feeling equal measures of magnetism and strain.

'You didn't think I'd want to?'

Thankfully Jack, Alice and Billie appeared before she could answer. Sophie made introductions all round. They had all worked hard for this weekend to throw Casuarina Downs open to the public, and she wanted everyone to be acknowledged, for she certainly could not have accomplished the preparations alone.

Jack hefted some of the bags and headed for the house. Charlie loaded himself up and followed.

This was the first time the homestead was full. Sophie discovered it enveloped them all with open arms. For this weekend, at least, she could see it had truly sprung to life and become a home, filled with laughter and noise, giving her a glimpse of what it could be.

Because the visitors were late and hungry, Alice immediately served lamb burgers and salad casually around the kitchen table. Amanda was comfortable and unconcerned but Anne was clearly appalled by the informality, requesting a knife and fork. To eat a hamburger? Good luck with that, Sophie thought.

Alice and Sophie had decided that the entire weekend should reflect the authentic lifestyle out here to complement their outback experience, so it was interesting to see how city newcomers reacted to the environment. Refuelled and brimming with energy, it was clear the children chafed to escape outdoors.

'I can take the boys out for a ride

around the property on the quad bike,' Billie offered, addressing Amanda.

One look at their broad smiles answered that question. 'Sounds like a wonderful idea,' their mother agreed.

'Okay, oldest first. Jacob, you come with me and we'll find you a helmet.'

'Can you take Drover for a run when you go?' Sophie asked.

'Sure.'

Jacob immediately became Billie's shadow lest he should miss out. The jillaroo enchanted the children. Everyone watched as they headed away from the homestead yard toward the outer paddocks, the boy clinging on behind, waving madly, barely visible beneath his safety helmet.

Charlie wisely offered to take Daniel exploring until it was his turn.

'Charlotte want to go.' The girl pointed to the cloud of dust as the bike and her brother disappeared.

'Oh honey, you're a bit small, but you can come exploring with Mummy. Is that all right, Sophie?' Amanda turned

199

for her endorsement. 'I'd like to have a wander, get a feel for the setting and where the accommodation is placed.'

Sophie nodded, then took a deep breath. 'Anne, this would be a perfect opportunity to take a drive in the ute out to the escarpment for the views that painters find irresistible. Then I thought we could go on to the billabong, which is a camping site and another inspiring scenic location,' she suggested. 'When Amanda returns we can change places, and I'll take her out to the cottage ruins.'

Although Charlie kept his distance, Sophie was fully aware of him, and he waved as she drove away with his mother.

Being confined in a vehicle together promised disaster with Anne, because Sophie still felt awed in her presence. But gracious though she was in every way, and dressed in designer jeans and a lacy silk blouse, she seemed to genuinely admire and appreciate the stark scenery. The amber and rust colours of the outback were more pronounced now with the approaching summer.

Anne asked questions and took numerous photographs. In a quiet way, a respectful acceptance settled between them, and Sophie believed her visitor was sufficiently impressed, which was promising for future artistic group bookings and workshops.

When they had almost returned to the house, Anne said stiffly, 'Thank you for showing me around. It's proved a pleasant surprise. I admire your pluck in wanting to live out here.'

'I appreciate your time. I'm happy to accept any advice or input you offer.' Sophie half-expected a barrage of disapproval.

'It all seems well-planned,' Anne said reluctantly after a pause.

Oh, good timing, Sophie noted, as they pulled into the homestead yard to see an excited Jacob scrambling down off the quad bike and Daniel impatient to take his place. Charlie lifted him up and clipped on his small helmet. Sophie's heart warmed to see him so comfortable with his nephews.

With Charlie supervising the children, Amanda headed off with Sophie in the ute — their target destination, the cottages. At each site, Amanda stood and spun a full circle, taking in the view of the partial or empty building, its ambience and setting.

'These will be marvellous,' she enthused. 'I know exactly what style would feel right, based on your folder of ideas, and the dealers who'll have exactly what we want. Second-hand and recycled character pieces to be restored, and the ideal chap to do it cheaply and efficiently,' she said briskly.

Sophie was impressed by Amanda's quick mind, professionalism and knowledge. 'A rustic influence,' she enthused. 'We should aim for simplicity and comfort.' She reeled off all manner of suggestions of which Sophie approved and could envision in her mind.

'Wrought-iron light fittings, ging-hams and florals, patchwork quilts.' Amanda sank her hands into her pockets and strolled. 'Open wood fire, rugs on natural timber and stone floors. Candles, comfy sofas, and above all big, soft beds with lots of pillows. A perfectly placed vase of fresh flowers. Appropriate paintings on the wall. Aboriginal artwork?' She turned to Sophie for corroboration.

She shrugged. 'Alice is sure to know someone.'

'I'll keep everything in storage until you're ready to furnish.' She released a long, slow sigh. 'Sophie, this project is so refreshing for me to undertake. It reminds me of our grandparents' farm down south,' she said wistfully.

'Charlie told me about it. Sounds like you made some awesome childhood memories there.'

'I have *so* wanted this kind of country experience for our children,' she confided, settling on a huge smooth boulder, letting her gaze drift away across the view. 'Warren often misses out on sharing things with them. We've discussed it and he knows I don't want him to be an absent parent. Yet I know it's inevitable there will be times like this weekend where his work takes priority.' She shook her head. 'The time pressure on court work is enormous. I guess I'm hoping it doesn't become a habit.'

Sophie recalled Warren's ready involvement with his children at the Kendalls' recently. 'He'll be fine. Watching him the other weekend, it's clear to see he knows family is important.'

'We're both so busy, and it's too easy these days to be caught up in life and forget to slow down for time out.'

'The fact that you're voicing it means you're aware of any potential problem.'

'You're a good ear.' Amanda smiled. 'Mother's life has always consisted of being everywhere *but* home, except for entertaining. I love my career, and I'm in demand, but I'd give it up or pull back just like that — ' She snapped her fingers. ' — if I thought my children suffered.'

'I imagine it's tricky finding a balance.'

'True.' Amanda rose and they headed back to the ute, parked under a shady gum. 'We haven't discussed a budget.' Amanda named a ballpark figure. 'From what I've seen today and a quick estimate, it's doable around that range.'

Sophie breathed a sigh of relief. 'That's feasible from my end.' It meant not digging too deeply into the bank balance.

By the time Sophie and Amanda returned to the homestead at twilight, everyone had congregated in the kitchen. The boys played dominos with Billie on the floor, while Charlotte sat on a stool between Charlie and Anne, each drinking a glass of wine.

Sophie was reminded of her own family get-togethers in Western Australia, and full houses when the Nash clan all gathered at Sunday Plains. She only realised now, stepping into the kitchen with Amanda, the aroma of cooking meat and baking damper wafting across to them, how much she missed those sociable times.

Billie jumped to her feet, smiling and lively as always. 'Jack will be over shortly. Everyone has been allotted rooms.'

She must have read Sophie's mind, and she blessed the girl's fresh youthful presence around the place. 'Great.' She caught Charlie's soft gaze watching her as she pulled out her pony tail, shook her hair free around her shoulders and said, 'If you'll all excuse me, I'll go hit the shower and be back in fifteen.'

Because the Kendall women were always so stylishly dressed, Sophie felt pressure to make more of an effort than normal with her appearance for dinner. Although she would have been perfectly content with a fresh pair of jeans and shirt, she rifled through her wardrobe and produced white slacks and a silky hot-pink over-shirt. She simply brushed her long hair and left it loose.

When she reappeared, Amanda had freshened up and changed, too, and knelt on the floor playing with the children. Billie and Jack leant against the counter drinking beers.

'Everyone have a good afternoon?' she approached, feeling awkward because Charlie kept staring at her. If he was comparing her to Belle, she would fail. A general positive chorus and smiles were her rewarding replies.

Charlie slid off his stool. 'Wine?' he murmured as she moved to help Alice serve up.

She nodded. 'Thanks.' The atmosphere between them was polite and formal. She couldn't help feeling genuine regret at the loss of their former intimacy.

Alice's feast proved a spectacular winner. The table was rustically set with gum leaves and simple fat white candles. Jack flicked his cigarette lighter over the wicks. Knowing his secret, Sophie couldn't help watching his dynamics with Billie all night, longing to tell him she knew.

In her own situation, she couldn't help feeling guarded with Charlie around, and it bothered her because, despite their distance, she still really liked him. More than she should. And she wondered if her feelings would ever fade.

Sophie helped Alice plate up. They had given the children a simple lamb stew but for the adults, the main course was kangaroo stew with its distinctive strong gamey flavour, cooked in red wine, served with a sweet potato and pepper mash and a side of steamed vegetables.

By the time everyone was seated and served, Sophie assumed her place at one end of the table to discover Charlie seated on her right.

She worried how their choice of meat would be received, especially by Anne, whose gourmet tastes and opinion would be important. But the food was complimented upon and accepted. The children chattered delightfully through-out, especially Charlotte, who ate everything on her small plate and mopped up the gravy with a slice of damper.

'This meal,' Sophie told them, 'is just a sample menu of the type of food we plan to serve homestead guests. There will also be such items as fresh yabbies, grilled barramundi, roast lamb, lemon myrtle and wattleseed cakes, trifle, pavlova. Pretty much the more tradi-tional and renowned Australian fare.'

By the time the trifle dessert was served and eaten, one small girl was rubbing her eyes and two boys had grown quiet. Amid thanks to Alice, Amanda bustled them all off to bed. When she returned, she made her excuses and retired, too. After coffee and a quiet chat, Anne acknowledged the day with respectful thanks and also withdrew.

When Sophie had helped clean and tidy up in the kitchen, she told Alice, 'I'm going out for some fresh air,' hoping to avoid Charlie; but she was only halfway to the door when he rose from his chair in the sitting room.

'Mind if I join you?'

She longed to say *No, I'm drawn to you and it frightens me*. She frowned in surprise, for they had sidestepped each other all afternoon, their conversation during dinner seated next to each other polite and incidental.

'Just going to check on Drover. He's been neglected lately.'

Charlie's dark wry glance almost said *I know the feeling* and she cringed. Walking alongside him in the dark across the yard, with the warm night air stirring the dry gum leaves, she took herself in hand and almost felt that familiar comfortable ease with him again. Except she had no idea of his thoughts.

They checked on Drover, made sure he had water and was given a liberal dose of affection, then turned back to the homestead.

Sophie knew the silence couldn't last

and she tensed when Charlie sought her hand and murmured, 'Still no response?'

He was still interested? She paused and faced him in the semidarkness, the golden homestead lights spilling only a short distance out into the gloom. Her heart pounded. She had been dreading this moment.

'I *do* care for you, Charlie. More than I care to admit.'

'Then why — '

She gently placed a finger over his mouth. How could she so cruelly deny the person she loved? How could she be so heartless? She adored this man. A gust of wind whipped hair across her face and he tenderly tucked it behind her ear.

'You looked very comfortable with Belle.'

'Belle's comfortable with everyone. Besides, I thought I'd already explained she wasn't for me.'

'Oh Charlie,' she sighed, grateful to hear it but confused. 'I'm not turning you away. I can't . . . I just don't seem able to move into a deep relationship.' This was as much as she had admitted to anyone.

'Why not?' he whispered, drawing her against him.

She knew the answer, but to voice it was difficult and the hardest private admission she would ever have to make. Feeling wretched and close to tears, Sophie shook her head, broke contact and began walking away.

'Sophie — ?'

'Charlie, please.'

'No. I accept your problem, whatever it is. For now. I have something else I need to tell you.'

Sophie stopped and half-turned to listen. He closed the distance between them and sank his hands into his pockets. Facing the house, the light from indoors glinted off his glasses. 'I'm going away in the New Year for a couple of months. A geology trip to Hawaii.'

'Oh?'

Sophie wondered if this was a sudden

decision, a reaction to her apathy and Charlie's way of gently ending their relationship or at the very least putting it on hold. Months, he said. Virtually the whole summer.

Trying to sound positive and happy for him, she said, 'Lovely destination.'

He nodded. 'They're islands of great volcanic beauty and are still evolving, which makes them all the more fascinating. Our planet offers many more that take your breath away.' He tilted his gaze to the stars.

In the dim light, she braved a glance across at him and sensed an uncertainty about him. 'I hope you have a great trip.'

'I'll be back for the start of the new university year, but it's too good an opportunity to miss,' he explained gently.

'I can imagine,' she agreed generously. *I get it, you're dumping me.* She stifled a building ache inside. If he intended to end their relationship, it was probably best to do it now. She couldn't give him the commitment he sought, so he had that right. But it didn't make the break less painful. No previous parting had ever left her feeling this desolate.

The wind rose again and she shivered. 'See you in the morning.' She quickly spun on her booted heels and strode for the house.

* * *

On Sunday morning, everyone slept late. Even Sophie. So when she shuffled into the kitchen still barely awake, she and Alice, who was already bustling about, decided on a substantial brunch instead.

But soon enough small pairs of feet pattered about, trailed by their mother, stretching, looking elegant in her silky pyjamas. 'Morning,' Amanda yawned. 'That was the best night's sleep I've had in a long while. Even the children didn't wake. Those beds,' she raved.

Sophie laughed. 'After years of

sleeping in swags on hard ground, I made sure of comfortable beds here.' She explained about brunch. 'It's a beautiful morning so we'll set up outside. Half picnic, half barbeque. How does that sound? I imagine you won't want to be late getting away today.'

'Perfect. Come on, munchkins, let's all get dressed.'

Anne and Charlie appeared soon after, hovering near the kitchen, making themselves at home and drinking coffee while Alice mixed dough for damper and scones, and peeled potatoes for a creamy salad. Sophie beat the batter for pancakes and cooked them. When Jack and Billie arrived they were put to work setting up tables and chairs out on the lawn. At Sophie's invitation the boys readily agreed to accompany her to let Drover off his chain, and the children played happily until brunch. Jack took charge of grilling the lamb sausages and prawns.

Anne drifted about in the background, but when the boys returned flushed and hungry everyone took a seat around the long trestle table and helped themselves.

'We seem to be doing nothing but eating,' Amanda laughed.

'I can vouch for the fact that the outdoors gives you an appetite,' Charlie put in knowingly.

Keen-eyed Alice floated around them, tactfully serving mugs of tea and coffee.

'Sophie.' Anne caught her attention from across the table. 'Your hospitality here is of the highest level. What price do you plan to charge for overnight accommodation?'

A compliment? Sophie was speechless. 'I have absolutely no idea.'

When Anne suggested a price, Sophie nearly fell off her deck chair onto the grass in surprise. Charlie saw her shock and grinned.

'This is a five-star luxury experience. Don't undersell yourself,' Anne said reasonably while Sophie's mouth still gaped. 'People will *pay* for this. It's unique and only a day's drive from the city, so weekend visits are possible.'

Sophie was gratified to hear it.

'I have a personal group of friends who crave this kind of escape but prefer to do it in comfort,' Anne continued. 'On the other hand, some artist acquaintances are entirely bohemian and would be perfectly happy camping and painting in that magical billabong setting. Your choice of hospitality covers it all.'

'From what I've seen,' Amanda put in, 'the cottages will be somewhere in between. If you provide breakfast supplies and perhaps picnic hampers on request, those who prefer to be more independent can do their own thing within designated tracks on the property.'

The following hour passed too quickly. Sophie had thoroughly enjoyed the company and sensed a slight thaw from Anne. She would be sad to see the family leave. Charlie's departure meant something else entirely. Wine flowed

217

but Sophie noticed he wasn't drinking in advance of driving their entourage back to Adelaide. Drover had stretched out at Sophie's feet, obedient and watchful throughout.

'What time do you want to get away?' Charlie asked his sister eventually.

'Half an hour or so. The boys want to live out here,' she chuckled.

Anne had graciously endured the weekend but Sophie suspected the great outdoors was not her cup of tea. While she had been generous with her time and positive with her opinion and comments, an edge of boredom was obvious in her manner — unlike her grandchildren, who were enjoying every moment.

Sophie helped Alice clear up while their guests packed. Charlie restacked the roof rack and tied it down. He and Jack politely shook hands. Billie received high fives and beaming smiles from the boys, and then they were piling into the vehicle's three rows of seats.

Amanda embraced Sophie warmly. 'This is the best weekend we've had in ages. Next time, we're bringing Warren.'

Sophie's first return guests! She was delighted.

'I'll be in touch,' Amanda continued. 'I'm so keen to start searching and buying for you.'

'Sophie, thank you for everything.' Anne politely shook her hand.

The final goodbye was the one Sophie feared the most. Charlie solved the dilemma with a restrained, almost impersonal, kiss on the cheek before climbing behind the wheel. The touch and smell of him must last her for a long time. Perhaps forever. Was this one last tantalising memory?

Sophie pushed aside the building devastation at possibly losing the man she loved and the close friendship she had created with his family. So it hurt to smile and wave, enduring the aching knot in her chest as the vehicle slowly pulled away.

Over summer, the unresolved situation with Charlie haunted Sophie. Would she ever see him again? The possibility was unthinkable as well as unbearable. Billie went home to her parents for Christmas but was only away a week, although Sophie had told her she could stay longer.

In the New Year, when Charlie would be jetting off to Hawaii, work began in earnest refurbishing the shearers' quarters and existing workers' cottages on the homestead block. The three of them only worked mornings and evenings, avoiding the hottest part of the days.

Summer was fierce and relentless, but there was work to be done. The existing accommodation was swept out and scrubbed. Billie and Sophie whitewashed while Jack undertook repairs so that all would be ready by autumn.

Alice maintained packed lunches and coolers for drinks. She didn't have a proper vehicle licence but Jack taught her to drive the quad bike and she hurtled out to them wherever they were on the property.

The process of restoring the three cottage ruins further out would take longer. Sophie privately held doubts about the common sense in bringing the tumbledown walls and heaps of rubble back to life until Wally, a wiry middle-aged bachelor stonemason, arrived one day in his battered truck. He had written and expressed interest in the work, having heard about it via the local bush telegraph. Since his experience and references seemed sound, Sophie invited him to come out and take a look.

If she had judged on appearances, she might have turned him away, for he looked like a tramp in his ragged clothes and shaggy unkempt beard. But when she drove him out to the isolated cottage ruins on the property, he silently climbed out of the ute and squinted, standing reverent for a long while, as if imagining the past glory days of the small homes and the hard lives they had once sheltered.

He walked around, assessing, declaring each one a 'little beauty'. 'Take me mebbe six months to do 'em all,' he declared.

Sophie sensed a kindred spirit and smiled. 'Name your price. Job's yours.'

He grinned, they shook hands on the deal, and that was it. From then on, Wally became a fixture. He kept to himself, and in the heat chose to camp down at the billabong.

Sophie visited twice a week to deliver his supplies and whatever else he asked for. He usually produced a pencilled list on a scrap of paper with building materials he needed, and Sophie either had them trucked up from Hawker or drove down in the ute and picked them up herself.

Over time in the following weeks and with quiet caution, Wally told her he'd left home young and become a drifter. 'Doin' odd jobs for a meal and bed for the night. Twenty years ago on me wanderings I seen a derelict abandoned cottage and slept in it overnight. In the morning I took a good look at it and decided to give it some life again. Spent months restoring it. Learnt a lot as I went.'

Each time Sophie visited, she noticed changes. Rubble was cleared and neatly piled, support beams were installed. Wally's skills and hard labour worked the random stone using a hammer and chisel, and the lovely old stone walls slowly rose to roof height, ready for the roof timbers and slate. The shells were actually starting to resemble homes again. By summer's end, as crisp mornings overtook still hot ones, all three cottage shells were ready to be roofed.

Sophie investigated solar panels, since there was no electricity supply out here. Wally gave her the measurements and she ordered double-glazed timber windows. Her excitement mounted. Each cottage would be a delightful secluded escape for guests.

Wally predicted perhaps another three months until they opened to paying guests, but Sophie could finally see her long-term vision coming to life.

One evening as she typed up information and printed labels for the workshop heritage displays on her office computer, Amanda phoned. She had regularly emailed photos and updates on her buying progress. 'Judging by the pictures you sent, you're going great out there. I can't believe the ruins are half done. When did you want the first load sent out that I have in storage?'

'The homestead cottages and shearers' quarters are ready. I'm thinking any time in the coming weeks would be fine; then I can start advertising and taking bookings from April right through until shearing in spring. I can't handle anything after that.'

Amanda named a date and Sophie wrote it on her calendar.

'Heard from Charlie?' his sister idly asked.

He *had* sent emails, languishing

unanswered in her inbox. She thought he was just being polite and hadn't replied. If they weren't going to continue seeing each other, it would just make it harder later on if they didn't make a clean break now. If their relationship wasn't going anywhere, she would find it impossible to keep Charlie as merely a friend. Her feelings were too strong.

'Yes,' Sophie said eventually. 'Sounds like his trip is an amazing adventure.'

Sophie didn't pursue the subject further. Thankfully Amanda didn't press the issue and they hung up.

★　★　★

Then everything seemed to happen at once. Early autumn brought the first breaking thunderstorm and soaking rain, which was great for the property pastures and eased the exhausting summer heat. Charlie should be back from Hawaii and at university by now.

Within a week, Amanda emailed to

confirm a date when the truckload of furniture would arrive. Sophie was excited to be able to put finishing touches to the workers' cottages and shearers' quarters, which had all come up a treat with a lick of paint and lots of elbow grease.

On the day of the truck's arrival, Sophie waited impatiently at the homestead gate to meet it. Immobile with shock, she watched Charlie vacate the driver's seat and step down from the cabin. At first sight of him, Sophie felt like jumper leads were attached to her heart and she was kick-started into life again. She realised she had been operating on auto pilot all summer without him and that her feelings for this man were endless. And she was terrified. He was tanned, no doubt from all that Hawaiian sun, and smiling. In a word, irresistible.

In two long strides, he stood before her. He didn't bother to remove his glasses and he didn't muck around with a peck on a cheek. He went straight for her lips, knocking off her Akubra in the process, and kissed her soundly, leaving her breathless.

When they drew apart and recovered, he rescued her hat on the ground, placed it gently back on her head and asked, 'Did you get my emails?'

Sophie cringed and jammed her hands into her pockets. 'I did. It's been a busy summer.'

'I thought you'd forgotten me.'

The warmth in his voice and her melting insides tore her apart with the challenge to let herself fall in love. Feeling vulnerable, she asked quickly, 'How was Hawaii?'

'Inspiring and volcanic,' he chuckled. 'In every way.'

Sophie smiled. Charlie's passion for his work was contagious, breaking down her resistance and swiftly rekindling all the reasons she was attracted to him. She found herself listening with genuine interest as he made geology sound fascinating.

'Hawaii is on the Pacific plate.

Basically, it's a hotspot. The islands erupted from volcanoes on the ocean floor.' When she remained silent, he asked, 'Have I lost you?'

'No. You actually make science understandable.'

'Comes from years of teaching kids and trying to make it fascinating. Enough about my work. Amanda tells me you're ready to fit out some of your accommodation. You've been working hard and April's not far away.'

'It's all happening. Word has spread, and I've already had enquiries before the season's even begun. I'm open for business.'

'Pleased to hear your plans are going well.'

To deflect the impact of his steady roving gaze, she glanced toward the truck. 'How did Amanda convince you to bring this load way out here?'

'I'd do anything for you, Sophie,' he confessed softly.

She shouldn't have been stunned by his admission and generosity. 'I'm extremely grateful.'

'We only hired the truck for twenty-four hours to keep costs down, so we need to unload this baby. Jack around?'

Sophie nodded. 'I'll go fetch him and we can get started.'

Charlie parked the truck closer to the outbuildings for unloading. The men carted the heaviest pieces of furniture between them, with Sophie giving instructions where they went while she and Billie lugged in the lighter individual furnishings.

They stopped only long enough for one of Alice's stellar lunches and were done by dark. At dusk, with the lights on bathing the refurbished rooms in a warm glow, Sophie stood back and admired their day's work. 'Thanks, guys. Amanda has chosen well. This is perfect.'

Later they toasted their efforts — Jack and Billie with a glass of beer, Charlie and Sophie with wine, while sitting out on the homestead lawn, savouring the warm night air, a stirring breeze and the chorus of crickets. Drover sat obediently at Sophie's feet.

Charlie was staying overnight but had already mentioned he would need to be on the road again before daylight. When Jack and Billie left, Charlie walked indoors with Sophie and took the liberty of a gentle kiss.

'I'm a boomerang, Sophie,' he murmured. 'I'll be back.'

That was what she was afraid of, and in the morning when she woke he was already gone.

★　★　★

With the homestead accommodation outbuildings renovated and furnished, Sophie launched a tourism website, and definite bookings almost immediately began flooding in. There were even times, as she was busily caught up in the involvement of it all, that she could ignore her ache of loneliness for a while when it hit her unexpectedly. But in quiet moments it still caught her off guard. Her thoughts subconsciously flew to Charlie, and she faced the alarming realisation that she missed him.

*   *   *

Charlie frowned, deep in thought, as he drove to work each day. He strolled the university hallways and grounds, preoccupied. The cause of his deliberations: one Sophie Nash.

His mind came up with questions and no answers. Why did she remain so distant? Why hadn't a gorgeous woman with a sense of humour and huge physical appeal already been snapped up by another man? Must be something wrong with all the males out there in the world not to see deeper to that inner goodness and beauty she possessed. And that puzzling vulnerability in such a strong woman.

But then he got to thinking that maybe they had tried and, like him, been blocked. Personally, he wanted every other man to keep his hands off because he wanted her for himself. Except she gave off mixed vibes of attraction, then disinterest. If only he could break through that stone wall she had built. He was stumped why. Whatever the reason, it must have cut deep. He only hoped in time she would be able to dismantle that barrier and trust him enough to confide.

He was more than sure she liked him. Those soft, warm lips had kissed him back. Maybe all she needed was a little push. He mentally rubbed his hands together. Time for action.

He made a few telephone calls, set up appointments to meet people, and called in some favours to set his intentions in motion. He scratched his head when he was done. He was taking a huge risk and was probably crazy to burn his bridges but, where Sophie was concerned, he was playing a hunch. He'd worry about the consequences later. If the scheme backfired, he would try plan B, except right now he didn't have one.

He just hoped all the rain crossing the whole state lately didn't affect what he had in mind.

* * *

Sophie paced her office, glancing out at the sodden homestead yard running with rivulets after three days of wild lashing rain. From a lifetime of living on the land you learned to accept the weather; but as welcome as rain was out here, this was too much. With creeks rising, roads were cut and closed. Thankfully the homestead had been built by its original owners above the flood line. With a backup generator and food, they could ride out the deluge.

But so much for the planned opening of her first tourist season. This wet weather couldn't be worse timing. With drenching downpours and floods awash across the plains from high-energy creek runoffs coming down off the ranges, it could be weeks before the roads were repaired and open again.

Hence her frustration. Everyone on Casuarina Downs had worked hard to a punishing schedule all summer and autumn. Even the bank had been finally placated after she deposited the proceeds of a healthy wool payment. One less thing to worry about. And now *this*. She watched the steady heavy rain sheet down.

With great lakes of water on the airstrip Tony couldn't land, and all mail was delayed. Annoying when you were trying to run a business, but everyone else in the district was suffering the same fate. She had contacted the earliest visitor bookings and posted updates on the homestead website and blog, but the inundation was a boon and a curse at the same time.

Everyone was hindered from any outdoor work, so there was plenty of time to think and talk. Jack and Billie had finally and bashfully shared the news they had kept to themselves all summer. Sophie grinned, recalling their conversation in front of a roaring fire after dinner two nights ago when the rain had first started. She had been enthusing over their headway in tourism preparations, more to keep their spirits up in the face of the abysmal weather outside delaying its launch.

'Everyone's in the same boat,' Jack had said.

'We could sure do with a boat around here at the moment,' Billie quipped.

After a spurt of laughter from everyone, they fell silent. Billie nudged Jack, who leaned forward, elbows on his knees, hands clenched. He studied his feet for a while before he spoke.

'I'll need to be moving north soon. Just wondering when you can spare me.'

'I've already advertised. Have two jackeroos lined up and part-timers for the six-month tourist influx. Course, no one's coming in or out until the weather clears. As soon as it does you should feel free to go. Both of you,' she added, withholding a grin until they realised what she said.

The tension between everyone dissolved and their serious faces broke into smiles of relief. 'I'll miss you both.' Sophie rose and hugged them.

Seated on the sofa again, Billie snuggled closer to Jack and they held hands. 'It's only been a couple of months.' She gazed with open adoration at Jack. 'But we know. I realise we haven't said anything before now or given you much notice, but you know Jack. A hard man to convince.' Billie's eyes sparkled with love.

'Billie, you've become like family to me. I can't fault anything you've done for us here on Casuarina Downs. You're clearly very special for Jack Bryce to topple.'

He pulled a wry grin, accepting her teasing in the spirit in which it was intended with good humour. Well, better than it used to be in the past.

'If you're short of help, Kendall has a pretty strong pair of arms,' he said bluntly with a challenging gaze.

Sophie caught her breath and the happy smile froze on her face. 'He's just a good friend,' she said as calmly as she was able, although her heart raced.

'Open your eyes, Soph,' he drawled. 'You light up when he's around.'

Jack's honesty shook her up. Neither envy nor hurt laced his voice as it might have done six months ago. 'I'm happy for you and Billie, Jack. Don't worry about me.'

Later as they left, Sophie touched Billie's arm. 'Can I have a word?'

She shrugged. 'Sure.'

'Has Jack spoken about his life?'

She nodded. 'Cried in my arms when he did.' Sophie gasped and Billie nodded. 'Amazing that such a great bloke came out of such a tough childhood. I know he needs and deserves security in his life, and I promise you I aim to give it to him. He's the one for me.' She smiled. 'He's a strong, quiet man who hides his pain, but I plan on letting him know he's loved every day of his life.'

The women hugged warmly. 'Thank you, Billie. I know you'll look after him.'

Sophie stared out into the dripping starless night, Jack's teasing perceptive words still ringing in her ears, and found herself gripped with envy. If Jack's hard shell could be cracked, why couldn't she be so sure about Charlie, and heed the message her own heart was telling her that she had so far ignored? She didn't doubt her love for him, only her inability to let it go.

Perhaps because she had discouraged Charlie so much, the damage to their future was already done and it was too late for them. And yet he had hinted he would be back. Maybe there was still a chance for them after all.

*   *   *

Unbelievably next morning, the rain eased for a while. By evening the sun squeezed through an opening in the clouds, but only briefly. The following

238

day remained heavily overcast again.

Sophie, Jack and Billie donned rainproofs and gumboots to drive around the paddocks checking sheep. Most survived by scrambling to higher ground and the lower slopes of the ranges. They rescued those bogged in mud or stranded, but the following week demanded patience until the water slowly subsided from the roads and at least four-wheel drives and trucks could get through. All the same, it would be weeks before tourists could move into the region again, and Sophie spent hours on the computer contacting guests and shuffling bookings.

Only days later, she was surprised to receive a radio call from Tony enquiring about the state of the airstrip. Because it was gravelled ground, Sophie believed it might be usable again and excitedly drove out to give it a full-length inspection both in the ute and on foot. Apart from chasing off some wandering emus, she and Jack agreed it was sound and reported back accordingly to Tony. He arranged to bring in the mail and the list of extra supplies they needed two days later.

Everyone eagerly awaited his arrival and scanned the clearing skies. He would be their first contact with the outside world in weeks. Sophie spied it first, the weak sun glinting off its wings.

'Oh blast,' she cried out in alarm as she spotted a pair of emus loitering at the far end of the runway.

Jack took off on the quad bike to frighten them away while Sophie radioed Tony in the air in warning. The plane aborted its approach and went around again. As it swept low, she thought she saw a passenger. People sometimes used his service to access station properties and tiny isolated outback towns. Maybe it was a reporter seeking a first-hand look at the floods.

On the second attempt, all seemed well. The emus had scattered further afield and Tony descended to land. 'Something must have spooked those birds again,' Jack noted, frowning.

Sophie swung her attention away from the turboprop gliding in from the opposite direction. One of the emus was running back toward the airstrip. It was too late to go chase it off again because it was too far away, and the Aero commander was almost on the ground. Sophie clapped a hand over her mouth and watched events unfold in slow motion. Tony must have seen the trouble ahead at the last minute because his wings wobbled, but he was committed to land and the aircraft touched down.

Sophie heard the twin engines throttle back, but the emu was madly running in every direction. They all realised in horror that a collision seemed impossible for Tony to avoid. She held her breath, almost unable to watch.

As the emu ran toward it, the plane veered off the airstrip, skidding sideways. Its wheels sank into the soft, wet earth at the edges and its nose jolted forward and dipped as it slammed into the ground and lurched to an abrupt halt.

Jack and Billie raced toward the plane on the quad bike while Sophie phoned their nearest Royal Flying Doctor base in Port Augusta as she followed in the ute. Instinct told her there was no way Tony and his passenger could have escaped injury after such a rough landing.

As they all arrived, flew off their vehicles and Jack heaved open the damaged plane door, Sophie stood behind him and gasped. 'Charlie!'

His eyes were closed.

'Charlie?' Jack said, gently shaking him. 'Mate?' When there was no response, he shook his head. 'Unconscious. Judging by the bump on his head, probably concussion.'

Tony moaned beside him in the pilot's seat, clutching his leg and wincing. 'Think I've broken something.'

While Sophie relayed information on the patients' conditions and symptoms under medical instructions from the doctor at the base, they assessed the men and prepared them for a flight to Adelaide. An hour later, a flight doctor and nurse had flown in and examined them both. Charlie had come around but sounded foggy and kept mumbling about 'plans'. Tony was given a pain-relief injection and his leg stabilised in a splint to be x-rayed later.

'With suspected concussion,' the doctor said, 'Mr. Kendall will need to be monitored for a day or so. His symptoms should improve in seven to ten days but we'll take them both down to Adelaide.'

Because Charlie was still vague and in pain, Sophie didn't want to bother asking him why he had flown out to Casuarina Downs. A short time later, the Flying Doctor flight took off again, transporting the two injured men to hospital in the city.

As the plane rose into the blue outback sky, Sophie's chest was tight with anxiety. Charlie had barely been aware of her presence because of his nasty blow on the forehead, which needed stitches. The fact that he had survived the violent landing, was alive and, like Tony, would recover, made a deep impression on her. What if she had lost him? As she had lost her father, her mother a beloved husband, and Dusty his first wife, Alison. Such a tragedy didn't bear contemplation.

Sophie called Amanda, who promised to advise her parents and be waiting at the hospital when the men arrived.

The accident was the catalyst to blow away all of Sophie's doubts. She was struck with the realisation that she must cherish every living moment here and now, not dwell on the past and let it rule her life. Why couldn't she have seen this before?

She immediately decided to drive down to Adelaide and see Charlie. All that mattered was her desperate need to see him and be with him. Sophie knew she would always regret it if she didn't tell Charlie in person how she felt. She had no firm idea if he still shared her affections; but even if he didn't, it would be worth the long trip just to see his face and assure herself he was going to be all right. As she packed an overnight bag, she considered the many times in recent months he had come to her aid, reliable and supportive. This time, she would be there for *him*.

★ ★ ★

After the long drive south, Sophie finally reached Royal Adelaide Hospital. Fortunately it was on North Terrace near the university, so she was familiar with the area from her previous visit. Ironic that she should return here, but it brought back lovely memories.

Sophie eventually found Charlie's room, took a deep breath and went inside. He reclined on a pile of pillows, forehead bandaged, minus his glasses, awake and with Amanda perched on his bed.

As Sophie entered, his sister turned and smiled. 'Here she is at last. Good timing. I was about to duck out for a coffee. Want one?' She stood up and grabbed her handbag. Sophie shook her head. 'See you both in a bit, then.' She disappeared.

At the sight of Charlie, Sophie's heart raced with a mixture of happiness and uncertainty. 'How are you feeling?' she stepped forward.

'Rotten headache, but seeing you I'm sure I'll forget all about it.'

She reached for his hand and grasped it tight, warm and solid in her own. 'I'm so glad you're all right.' She swallowed back her welling emotions. 'I don't know what I would have done if I'd lost you,' she whispered.

'I plan on being around for a long time.' He squeezed her hand.

'Why were you coming out to Casuarina Downs?'

'Why do you think?'

She looked into the depth of those compelling brown eyes and shrugged self-consciously at the warmth in his tender gaze.

'You honestly don't know?' he teased.

He still hadn't answered her question, and she wasn't sure enough of him yet to risk voicing her dearest wish and make a fool of herself in the process. But he was certainly giving off positive signals.

'Whatever the reason, you certainly made a memorable arrival.' She wrinkled her nose. 'Apologies for the emus.'

'At least it got your attention,' he murmured. 'Sophie — '

'Such a line-up for coffee,' Amanda said as she bustled back in. She glanced between them. 'Am I interrupting?'

'No, absolutely not,' they both chorused.

'Just spoke to the doctor again, Charlie, and no change. Still keeping you in overnight. Sophie, before you arrived, we were just working out the logistics of who can stay with him when he's discharged in the morning,' Amanda explained. 'I can do the day shift after I drop the boys at school, and bring Charlotte with me. But tomorrow night's going to be the problem. Warren's bogged down in the middle of this big case and he's always home late.'

Sophie guessed what was coming.

'I don't suppose you could help out for just one night? Stay over in Charlie's apartment in the guest room? Doc said it was a decent knock on the head and they'd prefer supervision for a day or two.'

In her rush to leave, Sophie hadn't considered accommodation yet. 'Sure,' she said, but with reservations. 'As long as Charlie approves.'

'I was hoping you'd agree. I won't be much company, but there's something I'd like to discuss with you.'

'Are you booked in anywhere tonight?' Amanda asked. When Sophie shook her head, she turned to her brother. 'Makes sense if she stays at your apartment tonight, too, doesn't it? Place will only be empty.'

'Absolutely. Keys are in my trouser pocket.'

Amanda found them and handed them to Sophie. 'It's getting late. The sitter's picking up the boys from school, but Charlotte might be fretting.' She leant over and kissed Charlie. 'See you in the morning after the school run, and I'll take you home.'

'Thanks.'

'Sophie, I guess I'll see you there.' She gave her a hug, waved cheerfully on her way out the door and was gone.

Left alone with Charlie again, Sophie was tempted to ask what he wanted to discuss but said instead, 'I should leave, too, and let you rest.'

'If you must.' As she shuffled awkwardly and made to leave, Charlie flashed, 'No goodbye kiss to help my recovery?'

Sophie spun on her boots and pulled a wry smile. 'You sound just fine to me, but if you insist.'

She returned to his bedside, leant over and intended to gift him a kiss on the cheek. Instead, a strong arm reached out and pulled her down.

She squealed. 'Charlie!'

Their faces were close together and their noses almost touched. She saw the devilish gleam in his eyes and a wicked grin parted his tempting mouth. So she kissed it. And he kissed her back. Sophie's heart sang.

'Probably need more of those tomorrow,' Charlie drawled. 'Strictly for recuperation purposes of course.'

'Naturally.'

Her feet hardly touched the ground as she walked back to the ute in the car park, Charlie's apartment keys safely in her bag.

* * *

Sophie felt like an intruder as she unlocked the beachside apartment. She found the guest room and unpacked her bags, then wandered through the living room and stepped out onto the balcony to admire the ocean.

She considered snippets of her recent conversation with Charlie. He said seeing her made him forget his headache, but she still didn't know why he had been flying out with Tony on the mail plane to Casuarina Downs, because he hadn't given her an answer. Just hinted she should know. Surely he wasn't coming out just to visit? But was that notion so preposterous? His kisses certainly cancelled any doubts on that score.

And then their conversation was just getting interesting, and Charlie was about to confide something important, when to Sophie's frustration Amanda had interrupted.

He had readily agreed to her staying overnight, and she would have to be totally dense not to pick up on his flirtation. She had tried not to show it, but she had been thrilled by his cheeky, playful mood despite being in a nasty accident only hours before.

Sophie sauntered back inside to the kitchen and checked out the pantry and refrigerator. Bachelor pickings, but she could get inventive. She whipped up eggs, added the few wilting vegetables from the crisper, and made a pan frittata. She carried her plate and fork back out onto the balcony to watch the sunset while she ate.

Later, she restlessly wandered the apartment again while she sipped a mug of tea, running her hand fondly over Charlie's glass jar of special collectibles, reflecting on what tomorrow would bring after Amanda brought him home.

★　★　★

They arrived later that morning, for which Sophie was grateful because it gave her time to tidy the apartment, after which she impatiently paced.

Charlie looked weary and unshaven but in good spirits. He had barely settled in when Amanda left again to do a food shop and stock up the pantry while her brother recuperated. She kept disappearing and Sophie wondered if she was being tactful in leaving them alone together.

Charlie ran a hand through his appealingly untidy hair. 'I'm going to hit the shower. I'd love a coffee and chat when I'm done.'

'Sure.'

She boiled the electric kettle in his shiny modern kitchen and poured their hot drinks as he emerged looking fresher, hair still damp and darker than usual, barefoot, a long white short-sleeved shirt hanging loose and casual over black cargoes. He looked so *good* despite his bandaged head.

He studied her up and down at length as he accepted the coffee. 'Thanks,' he murmured and indicated the deep comfortable sofa, sinking down beside her. He came straight to the point. 'You asked why I was coming out to Casuarina Downs. Actually I have a proposition for you.'

Sophie's heart skipped a beat in alarm. Surely not!

'Regarding Jack leaving, I think I can help.' Oh. Her hopes collapsed. 'I'd like to make an offer to become a silent business partner and invest in Casuarina Downs. I won't interfere in the running of the station, but I believe in you. I'm impressed.'

That certainly wasn't what she expected. She stared at him, blown away by his generosity. A timely offer that she desperately needed. Should she swallow her pride and accept? She noted Charlie had only offered financial support, nothing more. How would they work together on a platonic friendship basis?

'That's an amazing offer.'

'I'm not sure of the exact amount. Depends on how much I get for this place.' He glanced casually around the apartment.

Sophie raised her eyebrows. 'You're selling up?'

When he told her the estate agent's estimated sale value of his oceanfront property, Sophie almost slid off the sofa in shock.

'I want to invest it all with you,' he said sincerely.

'For that contribution, you would certainly be entitled to a full partnership.'

'So what do you say?'

'You'll be homeless. Where will you live?'

'I have my grandparents' farm down south on the peninsula. Amanda and I inherited it from them but she wasn't interested, so I bought her share.'

Sophie beamed. 'You own that special place now? You told me once about all the wonderful memories it held for you. Is that why you bought it?'

Charlie shrugged and in a rare moment of vulnerability, he seemed self-conscious to be so sentimental. But Sophie considered it a lovely tribute to their memory. 'So you're going to live down there?'

'Actually I think of it more as a holiday place than a permanent residence.' He returned their conversation back to business and said softly, 'If you're struggling with a decision because it involves you and me, and you're worrying how that will work, maybe we should talk about *us* first.'

'Us?' she croaked.

'No pressure, but just so you know, I've just given notice at the university.'

'You've quit your job *and* you're selling up?'

He nodded. 'If it's a choice between living alone anywhere without you, there's no competition. I'm looking for a place where I know I'm wanted. Where I can be content and happy. I was hoping it would be with you.'

'Oh,' she breathed, barely above a whisper, and her chest grew tight.

The challenge had been thrown down and the ball, it seemed, was now firmly in her court. Honestly, Sophie didn't doubt his feelings. He was making his interest plain. He had sent out a subtle feeler on the beach all those months ago, but he'd gone overboard now without talking to her first. What if she couldn't agree?

Yet the strong first attraction she felt for Charlie Kendall had grown into love. He was putting everything he had on the line for her. Talk about jumping off a cliff blindfolded. She owed him an answer and an explanation, but she had never confided her dread to anyone.

'You know how I feel about you, Sophie. It's called love and I'm in pretty deep. Boots and all.'

As Charlie had laid his heart open to her, his tender declaration brought tears to his eyes.

'Sophie?' he prompted, a clouded expression crossing his face when she hesitated.

The last thing she would ever do was hurt this wonderful man, but she remembered her promise of ten years ago.

'I love you, too, Charlie.' There. She'd said it.

'I sense a *but* coming.'

'I don't think I can do it,' she whispered.

He took her coffee mug and set it on

the low table nearby and clasped her hands in his. 'I have no idea what you're thinking right now. You keep stuff pretty close to your chest. I thought I was sure of you but, right now,' he continued, shaking his head, 'you have me guessing. What's bothering you?' he urged gently. 'I know you love me. You just said so. What's the problem?'

Sophie's composure began to crumble. 'Because it hurts, damn it,' she growled.

'So does falling off a horse, but you're supposed to get back on.'

She grinned. 'True.'

'Is this about your father's death?'

Sophie groaned and nodded. 'Partly. I know I was weak but after he died, I couldn't sit around to watch my mother grieve and see her world fall apart. So I split. Took off for the Territory. Worked hard to forget and save for a property of my own so I wouldn't need to rely on any man. That way I figured I wouldn't get hurt. Then, just when my life was coming together three years ago, I saw my brother Dusty's devastation when his first wife Alison was killed in a car crash.'

So far she'd been unable to look at Charlie while she spoke and pretty much mumbled to her feet. Now, somehow, she dredged up the courage to face him. 'I vowed I'd never fall in love. It was far too crippling. Foolish huh?' Charlie grinned, caressed her hair and let her talk. 'But I know now that we don't get a choice. Someone enters your life and you're destined to be together. I feel that so strongly with you, Charlie, that it terrifies me. I wanted it to go away but it wouldn't.'

He pulled her against him and she snuggled close. 'I watched my grand-parents grow old together,' he said. 'They were married for over fifty years. Sure, not everyone gets to experience such a fulfilling lifelong love, but I'll bet they knew sadness alongside the good times. Didn't ever look like they ever had any regrets. And I know they would still have considered it worthwhile if they'd only shared a few years together. How long were your parents married?' he suddenly asked.

Sophie frowned in thought. 'Twenty-five years.'

'Long enough to leave your mother with plenty of memories.'

'I guess.'

'Dusty moved on?'

Sophie nodded. 'He remarried to an Irish girl, Meghan, and they have a baby son Benjamin. But it took him years to recover,' she argued.

'Understandable. Overcoming grief takes a different amount of time for everyone.' He brushed a strand of hair that had fallen across her face with her head bent as she listened, and then tucked a finger under her chin, turning her toward him. 'I love you, Sophie and I want to marry you. Until death parts us,' he emphasised, 'no matter how long or short that time may be. I plan to be the man who'll always be there for you whenever you need me. When you wake up in the morning. Trust me,' he pleaded. 'That's all I ask.'

'You do have a way with words.' Sophie's doubt was turning to joy and, finally, a love she could set free.

He kissed her tenderly. 'Do you want me as badly as I want you?'

Sophie hedged, grinning. 'I'm thinking it would be foolish to let you slip through my fingers. It would hurt to walk away and not have you in my life.'

Love was so powerful, she discovered, it gave you courage.

'Pleased to hear it. So?'

'The answer's yes,' she announced breathlessly, but with the deepest pleasure.

Charlie beamed and sealed their commitment with a long scorching kiss that left her breathless and laughing. Sophie couldn't keep a smile from her face and Charlie looked equally smug.

She frowned and asked saucily, confident of her man, 'Why do you love me?'

He scoffed. 'Easy. You have hundreds of kilometres of wonderful rocky, geologically fascinating countryside out there that will take me a lifetime to explore. What's not to like?'

'You just want to go rock-hunting,' she protested. 'I'll never see you.'

He brushed her hair aside and whispered in her ear in a husky voice, 'I'm taking you with me and we're camping under canvas.'

'Softie. Who needs a tent? What's wrong with sleeping out under the stars?' she teased.

'We can do that, too. Whatever you want. Either way, we get to snuggle up together in a sleeping bag.'

'Drover might get jealous. When I go camping, he sleeps across my feet,' she chuckled.

'He'll have plenty of company when our children come along.'

Sophie sat up and gaped at him.

'Eventually.' He grinned.

At that precise delightful moment, Amanda walked in, Charlotte chattering until she saw her Uncle Charles and launched herself at him.

'Do you remember Sophie?' he asked her gently, drawing the girl onto his lap. She nodded and smiled.

Meanwhile Amanda was keenly observing the two adults looking dreamily at each other. She dumped the groceries on the kitchen counter and appealed hopefully, 'Please tell me you have some news.'

Two foolishly grinning faces were pretty much a giveaway. With his free arm, Charlie hauled Sophie possessively against him. 'Which lot do you want first?'

'There's more than one?'

Charlie and Sophie kept Amanda waiting while they kissed.

'Oh come on you two, there's plenty of time for that.' She planted her hands on her hips. 'Don't keep me in suspense.'

'I guess the best news is that we're engaged.'

'I knew it!' Amanda squealed and dashed over to hug and kiss her brother first, then her future sister-in-law.

Charlotte clapped her hands. 'Charlotte's happy, too.'

Knowing the child had no idea why and was responding to her mother's delight, they all burst out laughing.

'The second-best news is that Charlie and I are becoming business partners, too.'

'I'm selling up this place and investing in Casuarina Downs.'

'You haven't wasted any time.' His sister sounded impressed. 'When's the big day?' Her eyes widened eagerly.

'Heavens, we've only been engaged ten minutes.' Sophie laughed.

Charlie looked down at his fiancée. 'That's up to the bride,' he drawled. 'But as soon as possible?'

Sophie nodded. No use prolonging the promise of utter happiness.

* * *

The late autumn day two months later shone crisply clear beneath a weak sun. Sophie's only regret on her wedding day was not being open to love sooner and delaying her bliss in standing beside Dr. Charles Michael Kendall in front of a celebrant on the beach, about to commit her life to him.

Streamers stirred by an onshore zephyr fluttered from tall white poles around them. Their guests stood in soft sand. Standing closely around them to witness the happy day from outback Western Australia was Sophie's mother Elizabeth Nash; sister Sally; Phil, Oliver and toddler Emily; her brother Dusty; Meghan and baby Benjamin. Charlie's family were all there, too; including Michael and Anne — the latter still with reservations. Also Amanda and Warren with their three lively children, Jacob, Daniel and Charlotte. And the day would never have been complete without newlyweds themselves, Jack and Billie Bryce down from Gulf Station in the Territory, beaming with happiness.

The ceremony itself was brief, sealed with the simple slender gold ring

Charlie slid onto Sophie's finger that nestled so beautifully beside the sparkling pink sapphire he had found on one of his recent geology forays and had fashioned into an exquisite faceted solitaire. The bride wasn't wearing pink today, but she had chosen the creamiest shade of ivory for her slender lacy gown.

'You're mine now. Forever,' Charlie murmured after they had spoken their vows, and he almost took her breath away with a crushing passionate kiss.

Sophie loved the sound of that and all it promised. 'I know,' she whispered and kissed him back twofold.

She knew this man would be beside her every single day and no longer worried what tomorrow might bring. Whatever happened, they would face it together. For she had finally allowed herself to love and be loved, her demons conquered at last.